Non-stalgia

Edited by
Ryan Everett Felton
&
Summer Jewel Keown

NON-STALGIA. Collection copyright © 2021 by Ryan Everett Felton & Summer Jewel Keown. All rights reserved. No part of this book may be used or reproduced in any manner whatsoever without written permission except in the case of brief quotations embodied in critical articles and reviews. For information, email nonstalgia.fiction@gmail.com.

First MedusaFish Books edition published 2021.

Cover design by John Ilang-ilang

ISBN: 9798760593917 (paperback)

Thank You to Our Backers

Jay Carr

Calvin Duffus

Paul Evans

Marla Felton

Jonny Fruits

Tam J Guy

Tracy Heaton de Martinez

Jesse Michael Helm

Laura Hohman

John Ilang-ilang

Ana Ingles

Daniel Arthur Jacobson

Bill Keown

Suzi Keown

Nicole O'Neill

Sarah Olmstead

Polina Osherov

Gary Reiter

Jennifer Roo

Marc Rouleau

The Scaleekes

John Scalzi

Brandon Schaaf

Laura Sievert

Katie Snider

Lucy Snyder

Ashly Stewart

Denise Triest

Emily Warden

Mia Witzenman

Tim Witzenman

Anna Wolak

Table of Contents

Thank You to Our Backers 3
Table of Contents 4
Introduction 5
Carpe Lucem 7
More Crowns 14
Presumption 32
Fireflies 36
Runoff 43
Symmetry 66
Motivation 70
Heaven's Helipad 86
Blonde Nostalgia 90
The Night-Doings at Leroy's 101
Tunnel of Love 117
The Trees on My Street 127
Cause of Depth 142
Working Title 155
I Traveled This Far Because I Love You 168
About the Non-stalgia Authors 173

Introduction

If truth really is stranger than fiction, why do we continue to ask ourselves, "What if?" *What if I'd gone on that summer adventure? What if I'd asked out so-and-so? What if I won the lottery?*

And, of course, everyone's favorite:
What if we started a fiction anthology?

We decided to find out—not just that last one, but *all* the fictional wrenches willing authors would throw into the machinery of their memories. That's what we call *Non-stalgia*: Real life, but with fictional garnish. Autobiographical fanfic, if you like.

We asked writers from everywhere to share a personal moment, big or small, and then let their imaginations run wild.

We had no clue how authors would interpret the theme. Was there unsolicited erotica? You bet. But that's another volume. *This* book represents the best surprises, chuckles, heartbreaks, and scares in stories submitted from all over the world.

You'll find diverse genres and settings here, from the everyday to the madcap, 90's punk shows to unholy rituals. Each author has included a brief note about the event that inspired their piece.

Before we dive in, the editors want to thank those who made this project possible. We do *not* want to know "what if" you hadn't entered our lives. Thanks to the authors for sharing their pasts and their imaginations with us. To John Ilang-ilang, who designed the absolutely perfect cover art, we are truly grateful. Thank you to everyone who backed this project and supported original fiction. And thank you—yeah, *you*—for reading this book in a time when it's simpler to just scroll on our phones. (And if you're reading this on your phone, well... Carry on, you're doing it right).

Now. Turn the page and enjoy the worlds of *Non-stalgia*.

Ryan Everett Felton & Summer Jewel Keown
Editors

Carpe Lucem

Sarah Layden

After the rains, the neighborhood was made of pieces gone missing, remnants of a drowned culture. Where once there was Sunday leisure and *crème brulee* French toast, now there are rats and cement. Now I have my two boys, alone, the three of us foraging up and down a trail where trains once ran. One day, we eat berries. Another day, tree bark soup.

After the rains, the paving companies built walls over the old orchards. At first people tried to pretty up the cement. They painted murals that led us in the direction of a story that didn't make sense. A mermaid swimming in the sky. An apple tree with faces instead of apples. A cartoon dinosaur trumpeting the speech bubble, "If you can read this, you're probably alive. *Carpe lucem!*"

The bigger boy had sounded it out. "That's a fish," he said.

"No," I said, distracted by his brother, who dug his small heels into my side. "It's Latin."

"Carp," he said, "is a fish. What's 'lucem?'"

"Look at those clouds," I said. I tugged his hand to step around a dead bird with maggots for eyes. My oldest searched the completely gray sky made up of one cloud.

The murals have been painted over. The dinosaur had been bright red; now the wall is coated in dark gray. Now I lead my sons, one by the hand, one strapped to my back. We could crawl through the storm drains if we had to, but I hoped we wouldn't have to. I would have to carry both boys. We would stay in the open as long as the air made it possible.

The vegetable seller sat in the shade of a sycamore, packaging small crates of peas. His meat smoker, once employed in the daily roasting of a hog, now tumbled compost. We used to walk here for dinner, the sky the color of sherbet, the babies drowsy on our laps while we ate pulled pork. His market had closed long ago, after the trucks stopped bringing canned goods, boxes of cereal and crackers, all-natural soda. Bright cardboard packaging we'd carefully fold and place in our blue recycling bin.

I remember seeing the blue bins floating down the wide street, carrying not recyclables but children, the parents trailing behind, water up to their waists. Then we saw bins with just children, no parents. And then empty bins, tipping over and filling with water. Eddie went to help. On the roof, the boys and I sheltered under a plastic tarp. It didn't keep us dry, but it hid the view of the street and the bins and the facedown children, some of whom probably had gone to the same cooperative preschool as our boys.

My boys. Eddie has been missing since last spring.

Everyone we know has left the neighborhood. We should, too. But this is where Eddie left us, and where he'll know to find us.

My older son yells, "Mom, look!"

He tugs my hand; I follow. We haven't seen this brick building before. It must've been hidden by the latest copse of trees to be demolished, first by the insects, then by the pavers. You heard the rumble each afternoon. Nothing was being built, only flattened.

A large bay window juts from an old storefront, its contents dry and pristine. Through the glass are faded nautical maps and gleaming trophies. A small plastic box sits atop a shelf, a steel lock clamped down on its latch like a finger to lips.

Non-stalgia

My boy gasps. "It's treasure." The baby on my back, two years old and barely talking, points and says the word he always says: "Da."

On the trail, the storm drains gurgle. The last rain was two days ago, and still the water rushes through. I shush the baby, but his brother shakes his head.

"He recognizes it," he says. "It's Daddy's."

I don't know what to say. Eddie did magic tricks for the kids, twirling silver coins through flashing fingers—months of practice, quarters plinking across our bungalow's hardwoods while the boys slept. They begged him to reveal how he could make objects disappear. I've never seen this treasure chest before, but maybe it was something he made disappear from me. I swallow the lump in my throat.

Through the window we see shadows, movement. Before I can run, the door opens. It's James, who owned a piano store a few blocks away, distinct in thick-framed eyeglasses, gray hair askew, saying hello to everyone who passed. Now he has only one eyeglass lens; the other side is empty, just air. He flinches a little upon opening the door, and at first I think it's the light, the missing lens, or fear. Then I remember myself, and what we must look like. Smell like.

"I'm sorry," I say. He waves us inside without a word.

What we couldn't see from the other side of the window: a folding partition that hides another room. Twinkling white solar lights hang in mini-apple trees with fragrant sweet blossoms. A bistro table with four chairs, and place settings set for tea. Linen napkins, saucers and cups, a plate of cookies. My hand is on my boy's shoulder. He twitches with excitement at the cookies.

You have to understand that we have not been inside a restaurant or sat at a table for a meal in over a year. James motions us over. "Tea is almost ready," he says, as though he has been expecting us. He tucks one finger under the baby's chin and makes a razzing sound. He would have been an excellent piano teacher.

He reaches into the display case and pulls out the treasure chest. The small wooden box fits neatly in his palm.

"Just a trinket," James says. "I hold onto things for people, sometimes."

"Da," says the baby.

When James opens the lid, I'm disappointed that it's only paper, a small folded slip, instantly recognizable as from a fortune cookie. He passes the box to me. The fortune reads:

You will go on a journey. Pack light.

Pack light. Eddie forever was saying this to me, as I stuffed suitcases and duffel bags for family vacations, and later, when I thought we'd all be leaving for good with our things. We left; our belongings stayed. We've stopped going back. The black mold had crawled up the walls, covering our lives.

Non-stalgia

But the fortune, I knew, was something Eddie learned when he was in Scouts. "Pack light" was Eddie's way of saying I'd need light. Pack a flashlight.

I flipped the fortune over. Instead of a Chinese word, it offered one in Latin. "*Lucem* = light."

Right then, I knew: That's my husband in that box. His voice, his message. Urging us to keep going. James studies me. I'm moving fast, and I grab the boys and head for the door. My older son crams one last cookie in his mouth.

"We have to go," I say. "Thanks for the cookies. Thanks for this."

"Wait," James says.

In his hand is a flashlight. I test it, and the batteries work. The glow emanates from my hand. I imagine finding Eddie, telling him, *I can do magic, too.* The thought buoys me, the best trick of all.

INSPIRATION

This story started on the many walks along the paved multi-use trail near my old house. What had been in the neighborhood before we lived there? What would come after we were gone? And *when* would we be gone, and how? Mysterious business, that, and something that is often on my mind. As for the rain, there was one particular summer day when I went out for a run, and a downpour hit. Flash floods. I was totally unprepared. Soaked within a minute. My husband and kids came after me in the car, to pick me up. They'd brought towels. Then I started to reimagine the details of what had happened, and this story emerged.

More Crowns

C.T. Lisa

I'm a little less than reliable when it comes to, you know, like, the essentials. The yearly stuff, the check-ins. I don't know. I tend to avoid things.

The last time I tried to go to the dentist wasn't exactly a pleasant experience. I was in college. I hadn't been in probably six years, but I'd been flossing religiously and figured that would be enough. My grandma had been a dentist and was always going on about flossing. Truth be told, I only went because, being on the school football team and all, we had a pretty decent dental plan. That was part of the whole scholarship thing—they gave us insurance. They considered it a job, I guess. Perks and benefits and all that. Not that we understood how it all worked, or anything.

It all started when Coach gave us the afternoon off the first week of the semester to go get all of our visits taken care of.

"Go get those chompers trimmed, Big Time!" he barked at me. He smacked my behind with questionable enthusiasm and handed me a very unofficial-looking white envelope with my name written on it in green colored pencil. He nodded me toward the office door and motioned the next player in. I stepped out into the hallway. The rest of the team was lined up against the wall in a kind of ad hoc assembly line, nobody talking to each other; just a bunch of faces, isolated, texting or staring off. I turned a corner and opened up the envelope, which wasn't actually sealed. The flap had been tucked in. I set my backpack down next to an inoperative water fountain. The custodial staff had taped a piece of yellow legal paper over it that simply read, "Please Do Not." It seemed like a sufficient warning.

I pulled my phone from my backpack and called my grandma to ask her how dental insurance worked.

"Who's your carrier?" she asked.

"'DMO,'" I told her, reading the card. "Wasn't he a rapper?"

"That's the plan type, honey. The carrier, the insurance company—Aetna, Blue Cross. Who carries your policy?"

"What side is that on?" I was holding the card up in the air like a rare gem, squinting. "I can't read this fucking thing. The font is microscopic."

"Language, honey."

"I feel like I'm examining a clue from *The Da Vinci Code*."

"Please don't mention that movie to me. You know it makes me think of your mother. That dreadful woman."

"What about that movie could possibly make you think of mom?" I pocketed the card and crumpled the envelope into a ball and shot it into the trash can beside the window. Two points.

"She's a lying profligate!" Grandma screamed. Then she settled back into herself. "Apologies. You'll have to excuse me, I haven't yet had my coffee. I'm sitting out by the pool, sunning myself, like the crocodile I am."

"You really don't have to go on about her like that," I said. "We're on the same side, pretty much."

"Do you know what I'm doing? I'm watching the little robotic cleaner scrub the pool—have you seen these? They snake their way around the rim, dragging a net. I'll set the coffee once it reaches the waterfall. After that, I'll check the PH level on the console by the garage. This is my routine now. I watch the machines. I'm needlessly old, honey."

"Well, you've earned it, G-ma," I said. Over the line I heard birds chirping, distant lawnmowers.

"You know, you really ought to be learning these things on your own, Big Time. I can't tell you how insurance works any more than I can tell you how Buddhism works. You have to take that journey by yourself."

"I just figured you'd know how to do all this."

"Good thought, but I never dealt with the insurance companies when I ran my practice. I'm just one person, you know. A human being. I did the dental work—drilling, scraping. I gave people crowns."

"Crowns," I repeated.

"Yes. 'More crowns than the Habsburgs,' I used to say. Which was funny, because of their notorious underbite. That family had the jaws of deep-sea vermin. Do you know about the Habsburg Empire?"

"Did they invent dental insurance?"

"They were an Austrian monarchy. I sometimes like to imagine I'm related to them, or the Bohemians. And not that Freddie Mercury character, speaking of teeth."

"I'm sure you made a lot of people's bites smoother."

"*Smooth* has nothing to do with it. Dentistry is a subspecies of mathematics, as is music. They're all the same discipline, as far as I'm concerned. Look. Insurance information,

Non-stalgia

your grandfather handled all that for me. So he would have been the person to talk to, God rest his soul. After that came your mother, who stole more money from my practice than Bernie fucking Madoff himself."

"Language, Memaw," I said.

"My point being that I truly don't know how insurance works. Or if it even works at all, for that matter. Based on what I read in the news, it seems like the whole insurance racket is bound to come crashing down pretty soon. But regardless, you're due for a cleaning, I'm sure."

"You still 'read' the news? Like paper?"

"It's coffee time. I need to go. Tell your dentist you don't want the fluoride unless they have bubble gum flavor."

"What?"

She hung up.

Did that bother me? A little, yeah. I was planning on just kind of winging it with the insurance—I mostly called grandma because I was looking to talk.

Anyway, I walked out of the athletics admin building through the back stairwell, which opened up to the quad between the athletics building and the medical school.

I always thought it was weird, us having a medical school. It didn't seem fair. To them, I mean. Those people were doing real work, scribbling up a damn storm in the front of their classes, and meanwhile here's me, way up in the tippy top of the lecture hall, watching *The Wire* on my laptop every day, sixty minutes at a time, with my hoodie pulled up to hide my earbuds. We were living in two different worlds.

Anyway—so I'm walking, two-strapping my backpack, ambling across the quad with my brand spanking new insurance card tucked inside my pocket. It was an overcast day; the sky was the color of dirty soap. Long-sleeve weather. It seemed like the whole world had come outside. The quad was always full like that, like a carnival. There were people handing out flyers for some kind of bake sale. There was a girl walking barefoot across a slackline drawn between two mighty oaks. She was wearing a black t-shirt and wine-colored chinos, rolled up to her knees. She had her eyes closed.

So, eventually, I got to the parking garage. Stepped in, took the elevator to the top where it's just the sky hanging low above you, no ceiling.

I walked from the elevator to the car, enjoying the view, the shifting breeze coming through the treetops, swinging my lanyard like a security guard. I look over and, leaning up against the passenger-side door of my car, I see Katrina, this smarty-pants girl from my Tuesday/Thursday economics class. "How's the air up here?" I called to her. The place was deserted.

Katrina looked at me, she seemed concerned. She wore a purple beanie and a purple coat. It was the kind of conspicuous color coordination that makes a person look like a comic book superhero walking around in plain clothes. Her arms were folded. "Hey, Big Time," she said. "Please just listen to me. I'm in no mood for your judgement."

"Well how about my *spearmint*?" I raised an eyebrow and made a show of reaching into the pockets of my sweatpants as if I had some gum. I never carried any gum.

She gave me a quizzical look. "Listen, I'm serious. I've been rehearsing this speech in your car mirror for the last fifteen minutes."

"How did you know I was coming?"

"I know your schedule. But not because I'm creepy or anything. I'm a keen observer, it's what I'm all about. It's my major."

"You're studying to be an eye doctor?"

"No. International affairs. We observe economic trends and trade agreements. Anyway, it was Annelise, my roommate. She told me which car to look for. She said, 'it'll be an orange Ford Taurus—look for the car that's parked like a family of raccoons took it for a joyride.'"

She gestured open-handedly to my rear tire, which was admittedly a good two or three feet over the line.

Katrina went on. "Annelise was your lab partner in 'Intro to Meteorology' last semester, in case you don't remember. You gave her a ride home from class after that staged tornado drill."

"She had a very convincing shriek," I said.

More Crowns

We caught stray notes and rhythms from what I had to assume was the marching band practice, some ways off on the recreational athletic fields. The wind blew, pigeons fluttered, cars hummed down below. Katrina sighed, raking her hat down below her ears before she began to tell me why she'd come. "I'll start off by saying this," she said matter-of-factly. "I'm a human being, Big Time. Human. Anthropos, it's a Greek word. I'm halfway between the apes and the angels. A human. You believe me? And I made a mistake. A big effing mistake. No judgement."

"Did you fail one of those online take-home quizzes?" I said. "Don't worry, you can resubmit them. My tutor showed me how. He's one of those 'hacktivist' people, with the ponytails."

"This isn't about economics, you dingus."

"Hey, no need for that."

"Look, you and I, we don't know each other that well. All I know about you is that you helped my friend and you watch critically-acclaimed television shows on the sly on your laptop. This inclines me to think you have good taste and morals, a chivalric need to help strangers in grim situations."

I shook my head, like I was trying to be modest. Katrina took a long sip from her water bottle. I stuck out my hand, thinking she was about to offer some to me, but she just capped it and shook her head like an impatient bus driver. "I need a favor. There's no good way to say this, so I'll just say it." She paused to gather herself. "I've lost my sister."

I gasped.

She put an apologetic hand over her mouth. "Oh, no not like that. That came out wrong. She isn't dead. She's lost, missing."

"Oh. Lost," I repeated.

"Yes. Lost. Like that television show I saw you watching before you started *The Wire*. With Damon Lindelof."

"I actually kind of liked the ending," I said. "I told my grandma this the last time I saw her, and she called me a 'philistine.' What does that word mean, 'philistine?' Is that Greek, too?"

"I'm not sure."

"My grandma also described my mom as a 'profligate' on the phone. I assume it has something to do with her being an abusive alcoholic and a thief. I love how open I can be with you—I'm never like this. This is her car, by the way. Mom had to forfeit her license after she was institutionalized the second time. But she's out now. I think she's living in a trailer park upstate."

Katrina rubbed her chin and scrutinized me. "You don't seem like a child of abusive parents."

"'Parent, singular. I have many demons, Katrina. But trauma is in the eyes of the believer, as I always say."

"What, are you some kind of amateur aphorist, too?"

"I'm a fucking survivor, is what I am."

"Language, dude."

"Sorry."

"Look, the bottom line is that I need your car. Here's the deal: my little sister Talia was here on a college visit. She got in on Friday. I took her to a bar. I said don't judge me, okay? So, we had some drinks, we danced, we got debauched and rowdy. She ended up running off with a pack of goth-looking jerks while I was shooting pool with my poli sci TA, who is admittedly a bit of a flirt. Her name's Freddie."

"Mercury?"

"Talia has been missing since the weekend, so two days. My parents won't let her have a cell phone because she's only in high school and she's more than a little rebellious on a good day. Nobody knows about this, so please don't say anything."

I pantomimed a lip-clipping zip.

"But, here's where things get interesting," she went on. "We found her."

"Huh. You're natural police, are you?"

"No, it wasn't me. It was Annelise. She was coming out of the art supply store this morning and saw my sister hanging out in the parking lot with those same goth hooligans. They were handing out fliers to the customers, all of them wearing matching outfits. Black t-shirts and wine-colored chinos, dyed hair and all of that. You see, it's a uniform. Talia recognized Annelise and they all bolted into an alley. But Annelise took one of their fliers and did some digging. It was propaganda they were handing out, apocalyptic stuff—paganism, pragmatism, paranoia, et freaking cetera. It was a recruiting tool. They're a cult. My sister joined a cult, Big Time."

"Well, you sound calm enough," I said. "Are you sure you're okay?"

"I'm coping. I take deep breaths. There was an episode of *Gilmore Girls* where this exact thing happened, more or less. I keep reminding myself this to keep the panic from drifting too close. 'It's not real,' I say to myself; 'you're just trapped inside an Amy Sherman-Palladino nightmare.' By the way, you should add that show to your list, if you haven't seen it. Watch it after *The Wire*."

"Noted. So you need a ride?"

"Yes. I also might need your big dumb-muscled football body to use as a battering ram. It is a cult, after all. But we can evaluate that as the situation unfolds. What do you say?"

Here's the truth: I didn't go to the dentist that day, nope. Truthfully, I don't know how much intention I ever really had of going. I think more than anything I was just looking for a sense of accomplishing something, feeling useful. Katrina needed help and I needed a win. I wasn't recklessly eager or even particularly scared about the whole ordeal. I felt like I was agreeing to drop her off at the airport.

More Crowns

We got in my car. I curled around the spiral ramp and out of the garage. We drove over some speed bumps, passed the campus art museum and the library and the vet school, the cemetery. We got on the highway and headed south. She was guiding me, following some directions she'd written down in a spiral notebook.

"I've been meaning to ask you," she said in a voice that sounded more or less rehearsed. She didn't look up from her notebook. "Why do they call you that? Big Time."

"It's my name."

"No it isn't."

"It is."

"I sincerely doubt it. That isn't a name at all."

"It's my name, it's what people call me."

"No, it isn't a name. It can't be a name. It's, like, an adjective or something. Or a strata you have to ascend into—'the big time.'"

"I'm only a division 3 football college football player, if that's what you're getting at. Most of our games aren't even televised."

"You're telling me that this is written on your birth certificate? That you came screaming into worldlihood as a bright and red little polyp, and your parents decided to call you something as idiotic as 'Big Time?' Even if your mother is a bona fide dingus that still doesn't sound accurate to me. No. That's what your Coach calls you, isn't it? It's a football name. It has to be. It's simple, it has two syllables. He calls you 'Big Time' because you make big, timely plays—what's your position, anyway? Not that I'd understand."

"I'm the kicker," I said. "And speaking of names, what about this cult? Do they have a name?" I looked over my shoulder to change lanes. Katrina flipped through her notebook.

"They call themselves 'The Spawn of Habsburg,' have you heard of them?"

I furrowed my brow. "Only a little," I said. "My grandma was telling me about them this morning. I think they're Australian anarchists or something."

"Jesus Christ," Katrina gasped.

I reached out to hold her hand to comfort her, but she pulled away and smacked me across the back of the head.

We drove off into the maroon dusk. The sky was the color of squid ink and poison. We took the exit, wove our way around the shopping centers and car dealerships. We drove past a decaying laser tag studio that shared a parking lot with an adult superstore, turned left at a warehouse that sold swing sets.

Eventually, the street turned to gravel. We kept going at an even crawl until the way was blocked by some construction equipment. We parked the car and got out. We crept our way along the road until we made it to a wall of twisting trees. We found a path, tumbling down into the dark. We followed that as best as we could, going slow, gripping trunks, finding our way by snatches of light. We climbed over stumps and had our shoes sucked by muddy pits. I slid down a ravine and landed on a raccoon which stood up on its back legs and hissed at me like some possessed sock puppet before disappearing into the underbrush. But we kept going, through the brambles and the pines. Katrina ripped her shoe on some barbed wire buried in the dirt, but insisted we didn't stop. We crept into a cave. We saw an eerie orange glow in the distance. We neared it, closer. A fire and candles, and there they were, the Spawn of Habsburg themselves, a crude circus of twenty or so cultists. They wore rolled-up chinos and walked criss-cross slacklines strung above a massive tank of water. I saw crocodiles rolling in the froth beneath them. The walkers stooped and swayed. A vibrant male-female pair of what I assumed were twins took turns leapfrogging each other while a fit and mean-looking woman did a pike-stiff handstand on an adjacent line. They looked like some sinister family acrobatic troupe. The crocodiles snapped, the cultists bounced and bounded above. Some crawled like geckos along the wires. But no one fell or gave any indication of losing their balance. These were expert slackliners. I thought of the girl from the quad. Were they living among us?

As we watched the scene, I couldn't help but identify with these strange and diligent people. There was something helpless and desperate about it all, something reactionary. They didn't seem to be practicing rigorous discipline in their elaborate acrobatics—it was escapism, brazen avoidance. They had developed a method of distracting themselves from something—modern life, market culture, their vision of an apocalypse, whatever had been written on those fliers. I thought of my own gymnastic avoidances that day, the things I wasn't doing.

I turned and whispered to Katrina. "Look—if we're seriously going to do this, I'm gonna need a minute."

"Like fuck you do!" she hissed.

"Shhhh! Language, Katrina. I'm sorry, but I have something important I need to take care of. Just keep an eye on this, okay?" I gestured toward the slackliners, who appeared to be in the process of forming some crude human pyramid in the middle of the wire. "I'll be back."

I crawled out of the cave and started walking through the empty woods. I found a rock, and sat there for a while, scrutinizing the silence. I thought about my family. I thought about something that had been bothering me. Then I took out my phone. I dialed and I let it ring.

Look, I don't want to walk you through the whole bloody history of my relationship with my mom. Over the years, it shifted between being a fact and a fiction, let's just put it that way.

As the phone rang, I thought about our last fight. I wanted to take it back. I had called her up and asked about something completely inconsequential and erupted into some blood-thirsty version of myself and screamed at her. I'd called about filing my financial aid forms or my taxes or something. One of those mundane paperworky tasks that lurks in your periphery with the potential of leaving you feeling small and clumsy and utterly ill-equipped to grow into adulthood. I'd called her a "fucking fuck" and hung up. I don't even remember what she'd said to prompt it. Maybe the outburst had been lurking beneath my skin for a while.

My mom did some awful stuff to me. I don't know if I'll truly ever be able to forgive her. But I wasn't a delight to be around myself. I mean, a "fucking fuck?" What does that mean? Does it have meaning? It was a Molotov cocktail; I just lit the thing on fire and threw it at her. It was the kind of vicious bile you can only get across through pure dialogue. Who says things like this? What kind of monster am I? My mother is beyond unstable, she has a disease. Was I telling her to go and off herself?

Teeth. The visible part of the tooth, this is called the crown. It's just the tip, the part you can see—beneath the skin are the roots. Teeth are just bones out of hiding. There is what we see and the thing itself; roots and crowns, words and their meaning. My mother needed help, not hate. Not my half-chewed profanity.

Non-stalgia

But, of course, I didn't say any of this to her. Not in that moment as I called her in the woods, and not for a long time afterward.

Instead, speaking calmly into her answering machine, I simply said this:

"Hey mom. It's me. I was wondering if you knew what 'DMO' stands for? School gave me dental insurance."

I hung up. I padded back through the leaf litter and stooped my way into the cave until I found Katrina, crouched and eager, looking peeved.

"Ready?" she sighed.

"Ready."

INSPIRATION

"More Crowns" was inspired by my own tendencies of avoidance. Several strange and seemingly disparate events ended up lodging themselves in the wispy rear of my mind, culminating in this story—most notably, a wacky evening in which I was recruited to help a complete stranger find her debauched younger sister after losing her at a college party. I shaded around this central focus with exaggerations of a fight I got into with my family, as well as a recent trip to the dentist I do not hesitate to call "traumatic." Plus, like the main character, I also don't know how insurance works, despite having worked as a copywriter for an insurance company for 3+ years.

Presumption

Lindsey Danis

They have no idea how presumptuous it is to ask Jana to come a week early to unearth the boxes of Passover cookware from the basement closet and drag them up to the kitchen. They assumed she'd be delighted to have a hot meal; that she'd be sick of cooking for herself by now. When the invitation comes, buried midway through her uncle's email about the latest political crisis, Jana is surprised, then annoyed.

She brings it up to her ex-boyfriend, who recently returned from a trip to Thailand and wants to tell her how incredible it was. When he gushes admiration for the third temple at the great temple complex in Bangkok, she understands that this was not an invitation to reconnect, that what he needs, actually, is an audience. He joined a monastery in Isaan province and had a religious experience where he realized he hadn't been a very good boyfriend. He is matter-of-fact, reformed but unapologetic. "So would you go?" Jana asks, cutting off his description of morning meditation. They're at the not-quite-dive bar where the tables are covered with pennies, copper glinting beneath a sheet of resin. It's an upgrade from his apartment, where the living room was always occupied by roommates immersed in video games, a practice LSAT exam book askew on the coffee table, but it carries the aura of being his place, not one they shared.

***

Her ex looks older than he is, red-faced with a pale neck and light brown hair that's going gray at the temples, but it's different for men. She tongues the olive in her oceanic martini. The sensation is not unlike the one that arrives midway through the Passover seder, when the parsley has been dipped in saltwater, the matzoh has been passed around the table, the sweet wine is giving her a headache, and still there are pages of ceremony to endure and nothing satisfactory to tide her over.

***

Non-stalgia

He's on an abstinence kick, nursing a cranberry seltzer. She's had two drinks and craves another, but not here, where the familiar bartender pretends he isn't listening. "I get it. You were a crummy boyfriend," she tells him. "I never came from sex with you. If you didn't know, now you know." He gives her his full attention, waiting for her to continue, but he doesn't act contrite or particularly wounded by her admission. Jana runs a finger around the now-empty glass, conceding the point. It doesn't matter now.

***

"You can't ask for what you want, and you can't take what's on offer," he says with no trace of smugness. "The Buddhists have a word for people like you." His eyes shine with a private joy over his pearl of wisdom. He thinks this is a lesson—one of ego, not sex, though she'd argue the distinction.

Her uncle could get this way, too. Long ago she learned what was safe to mention at the dinner table. If he got going, he'd knock her like a loose tooth, like he was certain that with the right pressure she'd change her convictions.

She doesn't take it personally, her uncle's presumptions. But this she will not, she cannot abide. If she hears the word, she will obsess over it in moments when she is vulnerable: after sex with someone new, waiting for the bartender to notice her credit card on the bar, her nails clacking, her irritation rippling into *Jesus, am I invisible?* It would be the sort of thing you chew like a gummy candy forgotten in a pocket and unearthed, speckled with dirt, a dubious gem.

INSPIRATION

The seed for this story was in my-laws asking us to come down for Passover, but also to come down a week early to bring the Passover stuff up from the basement - they keep kosher and have 3 sets of dishes, including one for the holidays. We didn't go since we were seeing them shortly after and live 2 hours away, but I used my irritation as a flash prompt.

Fireflies

Keira Perkins

The two small sisters sat on the swings on a summer night. One small sister was very small, and the other small sister was slightly bigger. The bigger sister had hair like cornsilk, that tangled and blew wild in the wind. The smaller sister had eyes the pale clear blue of an afternoon summer sky. They sat facing each other on the swings, with their foreheads pressed together, whispering secrets; cheeks and mouths stained purple and their breath sweet from black raspberries. Dusk was falling with the smell of the storm on the horizon, electric and hot, but they were safe together in their own world.

Fireflies

The smaller sister spoke into the fading light, "Before I was here, I was a firefly."

"Before where? The swings?" asked the bigger sister. They had been running, barefoot, through the grass earlier. The bigger sister thought they were trying to see who was the fastest but maybe the smaller sister had been playing a firefly game instead.

"No, like *before* before. I was a firefly first, and then I was a girl. I don't remember what I was before I was a firefly." She considered briefly as she dragged her toes in the dirt. "I think I was a star."

The bigger sister leaned away from the smaller sister with her eyebrows knitted. "*No.* You were not a star. People aren't stars."

"I *know,*" said the smaller sister, as she kicked at dirt with a huff. "I wasn't a person. I was a star. Then I was a firefly. And now I'm a girl."

The bigger sister considered this. She did not remember being a star or a firefly before she was a girl on the swings. However, she did not remember many things. She had been a girl longer than her sister, but she could not recall life before her sister was there. Maybe her sister had always been here, and she had been a firefly before she was a girl, and a star before that.

"What did you do when you were a star?" asked the bigger sister.

Non-stalgia

"I shined so bright and hot. And I went 'pop! pop! pop!'" The smaller sister let go of the swing's chain and held one hand in front of her face. She made a fist and with every *pop*, she exploded her palm open like a small starburst. "You know? Like a fire. POP!"

The bigger sister considered some more. She thought she remembered being a fire once, but maybe not.

"How did you become a firefly if you were a popping star?"

"I popped so hard I flew across the sky," said the smaller sister, "And then I fell down, down, down and I hit the ground."

"And then you were a firefly?" the bigger sister asked.

"*No.* I was on the ground. I was so sad, and I cried. I missed the sky, but I couldn't fly or pop anymore. I cried so much all my fire got wet and it all went away except for just a teeny-tiny bit."

The smaller sister looked very small as she said this, but then she brightened and giggled. "It was my booty that was on fire just a teeny-tiny bit."

And she did a little wiggle dance in her swing, so she could shake her booty.

The bigger sister wiggled and giggled too. The swings started to sway, and then spin tight, and unspin, and spin again. They went faster and faster until the smaller sister cried out that she was so dizzy. The bigger sister dragged her feet along the

Fireflies

ground, grabbed her smaller sister's chains, and pulled her close. The smaller sister leaned back and wrapped her legs around her sister's longer ones.

"Okay" said the bigger sister, a little breathless, when the swings finally slowed and stopped. "And then what did you do? How did you make yourself a firefly?"

The bigger sister did not believe the story yet, not really. She still liked it. Most of the sisters' games were make-believe, but they still felt very real. That's why they were so fun. Sometimes they were gymnasts in the Olympics competing for gold medals; that game would last until one or both got hurt when they fell on their heads. Sometimes they were princess-horses and ruled over entire horse kingdoms… at least until they got bored and decided to kill everyone by throwing them off a cliff. Sometimes they pretended to be orphans and they would try to make a shelter under a pine tree. The shelters were never very tall and they fell down a lot; the girls were very small and only had sticks and pine needles, after all.

The smaller sister answered, "I wished, and I wished, and I *wished* that I could fly again. Then I saw the fireflies and I wished to be them." She laughed again and whispered, "Their booties glowed like mine."

"And then?"

Non-stalgia

"I wished so hard it made me a firefly and I grew wings. And I flew, and I flew, and I shined so bright. And I was happy again."

"But if you were happy as a firefly, why did you turn into a girl?" asked the bigger sister.

"I saw you running with the fireflies. Your hair shined so bright! And when you laughed it sounded like 'pop! pop! pop!' Then I thought I should be a girl too because you were just like me when I was a star. And we could be sisters together and you would show me how to be a star again. So, I wished and wished, and I wished so hard I *died*. Then I woke up and one day I was a girl on the swings, without my wings or my fire." The smaller sister said this all with urgency, the words spilling over each other. It was as if she feared they would be caught in her throat forever if she did not free them right now.

The bigger sister decided this was a very good story. It might even be true. The bigger sister had dreams sometimes of being deep underwater, her cornsilk hair flowing around her like seaweed. She had never been to the ocean, but she always woke with the memory of salt on her tongue. If she could taste an ocean that she had never seen, maybe her little sister really was telling the truth. Her sister had been a star, then a firefly, and now she was a girl on a swing.

"Okay," said the bigger sister, "but now that we *are* sisters together, what should we do?"

Fireflies

"We should swing high, like you showed me."

So they did, the bigger sister with legs like a colt and the smaller sister trying to keep up. Higher and higher they climbed in the night sky.

"How high can you jump?" asked the smaller sister.

"We're not supposed to jump. We could break our legs."

"You only break your legs if you fall. I am going to fly. I'll show you," said the smaller sister.

"Girls can't fly. We aren't fireflies or stars."

"Nah, they just don't want us to know we can fly. It's a secret."

The bigger sister saw her smaller sister's face was set with determination. She knew that face; the smaller sister would jump. The bigger sister knew she could not stop her sister, and with a thrill, she realized she did not want to stop her. They would jump together because sisters do not leave each other. The girls' legs steadily pumped as they climbed higher and higher. And higher still.

They looked to each other. "*Now!*" yelled the smaller sister. They let go of their chains and leapt into the darkness.

White-blonde hair reflecting the moonlight, peals of laughter crackling like thunder on the horizon. Small girls, and fireflies, and stars in the night sky, and no way of knowing which was which, or when (or *if*) they would fall.

INSPIRATION

My younger sister and I are separated in age by 607 days. When we were growing up, 607 days was sometimes forever, but it was still close enough that sometimes we would be mistaken as twins. When I think of my sister and when we were very young, I see us outside in the summer nights, chasing fireflies and picking wild raspberries. I remember our games of make-believe and that sometimes my sister would tell me she used to be someone else. We would argue because I thought she was lying and that she was trying to ruin our games with a trick. I wonder what would have happened if I had believed.

Runoff

Ryan Everett Felton

    Robbie and Elle were holding hands and pecking cheeks in the Camp Cross of Gold kayak shack when the call came in. Their walkies crackled in unison, echoed in the hull of the upturned canoe they used for a hiding spot.

    It was that new Head Counselor. Craig. "Calling all Lodge Leaders. We got a runner." *Krrrkt.* "I repeat, we got ourselves a runaway camper. Everyone hop to and start searchin'. Over." *Krrrzzt.*

    "Oh, no." Elle stood up right away. Robbie tugged on her twine bracelet from the floor. "Probably just one of the third-graders went for a pee. They'll find 'em. Stay a minute."

Non-stalgia

Krrrkll. "When I say 'everyone hop to,' I mean *everyone*." Craig's voice somehow became more authoritative filtered through fifteen bucks' worth of Radio Shack: "Camper last seen on the kickball field."

"Aren't *you* supposed to be on kickball duty?" Elle was now in a runner's stance.

Her boyfriend laid back. "I got Troy to cover for me."

Krrssht. Craig again: "Camper's name is Jesse Drescher. Fifth-grader from Lazarus Cabin. Spiky hair, big ol' glasses, 'bout four-foot-nothin'." *Krrrktz.*

Elle slid her fingers out of Robbie's, their matching purity rings making a little *tink* on the way. "Aren't you Lodge Leader for Lazarus Cabin?"

Robbie banged his head against a lacquered canoe seat. "*Yes*," he said. "Okay! Fine."

They both squidged into their Crocs. Robbie pressed his lips into the squawking radio. "Counselor, this is Robbie from Laz-Cab. The Drescher kid's one'ah mine. We're on it."

Elle slipped out and darted into the bushes on the left. Robbie counted to ten, then went for the trailhead on the right. It was a perfect system.

They took separate paths back to the kickball field. Robbie's campers were still there—minus one, of course—milling around, shouting for Jesse half-heartedly.

Runoff

Buck-toothed Stevie Flowers, the tallest, shuffled up with a red kickball tucked under his arm. "Hey, Mr. Robbie, where'd ya' go?" he said.

"Official camp business."

"Jesse ran away."

"Yeah, Stevie, I *know*. What d'you think my official business is?"

"But you left before—"

"Does anybody know where Jesse mighta' gone?" Robbie shouted. "Did he talk to anyone before he went off?"

The boys all shrugged or looked at their shoes.

Elle jogged up beside him. "One of the kids just told me Jesse's been sick."

"*Home*sick." Robbie spat. "Nerves, is all. I prayed with 'im. I gave him a Tic-Tac. What the heck more does he want?"

"I'm saying, Robbie, maybe we check the clinic?"

His mouth popped open. "Yeah," he said, nodding. "Yeah, he's got to've gone there. Thanks, babe!"

He took her by the wrist and jolted for the dirt road. "Everyone back to the cabin!" he shouted over his shoulder.

The boys looked at each other. A few started playing kickball again. A few headed for the lake. Only Stevie Flowers went back to Lazarus Cabin, because the others promised to meet him there as a prank.

***

Non-stalgia

"Yeah, the Drescher kid come through here, 'bout fifteen minutes ago."

The Nurse slurped her coffee. She had been the nurse since time immemorial, or at least since Elle and Robbie were first-grade campers—and they still only knew her as The Nurse. The shiny cursive logo of Camp Cross of Gold sparkled on her mug.

"Wanted to call his mom," she said. "I tell 'im no. Tell 'im, why don't you go back and play some kickball. He says he's sick, so I give 'im a Tic-Tac and tell 'im run along."

Elle squeezed Robbie's hand.

"Then the kid starts goin' on about he wants to… Whaddee say? 'File a complaint.' Asks where the head office is. I tell 'im, you're lookin' at it, Sonny Jim. File away!" The Nurse snorted. "Why, ain't he turned back up at the field?"

"No, ma'am, he has not." Robbie's cheeks inverted. Elle watched concern bloom in rosy patches on her beau's face.

The Nurse blew on her brew. "Ah, he'll turn up. Prob'ly just tryin' to steal some Mounds Bars from the canteen."

"I thought he had a stomach bug," Elle said.

"He's just *home*sick," Robbie and The Nurse said.

Elle looked out the window and twitched. "Wait," she said. "There."

"Huh?" Robbie joined her at the pane. She had the dust-encrusted blinds pried apart with a thumb and forefinger. He

Runoff

lined his eyes up with the opening.

"What am I looking at here, babe?" he said.

"There!" she said. "It's— There, it's him!" She tapped the glass. "Between those bushes, see?"

"Um…" All Robbie saw *was* bushes. Bushes and trees and dirt.

"Jesse's right there!" she said. She looped her arm into his and pulled. "C'mon!"

The wobbly screen door banged open and their feet clacked on the deck, then crunched in gravel. Elle led Robbie off the dirt-clod path and into a thick, green morass. They hopped over shrubs and logs. Batted vines and nettles out of their way. Huffed and puffed.

"Where we goin'?" Robbie said.

"I saw 'im!" Elle said. "He was right here."

"You sure?" he said, rubbernecking on tip-toes over her shoulder. "I don't see anybody out here. Can you—"

"Shh!"

And he heard it. A hefty rustle in the foliage. They tilted their heads and scanned, silent and breathless.

A half-dozen yards to the left, a dense patch of pure poison ivy shifted and fluttered.

Robbie nodded.

"Jesse?" Elle stepped forward.

They heard a gasp in the toxic greenery. A whimper.

Non-stalgia

"Jesse, it's okay." Elle pouted at Robbie: *The poor baby.* "We're not mad. Nobody's mad."

A pitiful little voice grunted through all that ivy.

Robbie crouched. "C'mon, bud. Let's go back to the cabin and talk. Like she said, you're not in trouble."

The bush went still.

Careful, Robbie reached forward. His purity ring caught the sun and made purple spots in Elle's vision. "C'mon."

Then the teeth clamped down on his fingers.

***

Head Camp Counselor Craig Kranszler would have looked stupid in his overtight Camp Cross of Gold t-shirt—except instead he looked like he could be everyone's dad, all at once. Though his belly jiggled in the juttering camp van, his chest was stone. A rusty mustache fluttered over his clenched teeth as he plunged a searching hand under the driver's seat.

"Watch the road, will you?" Next to him, Youth Pastor Tim drew up his thin pale legs.

Craig straightened, raising an eyebrow over his Aviators. He gestured out the van window, where the big white beast was plowing over untouched bushes and gopher nests. "What road?"

"Even so," the minister said. "Look where you're going. If you get us both killed, then where will we be?"

Runoff

"Don't worry, Father," Craig said. "I'd know these woods blindfolded." He yanked the bullhorn from between his legs and leaned out the window nursing it. "Jesse," he said. "If you can hear me, walk toward my voice."

The echoes of his call were buried in cicada song and van engine burps.

"He won't just come willingly," said Tim. "He's a troublemaker, that one."

"Who, Jesse?" Craig laughed. "He's a timid little nerd. I'd know. I was one, too."

"Causing all sorts of ruckus in the mess hall about 'there were no brontosauruses on Noah's Ark.' Like *he* knows better!" Tim snorted. "And now he's homesick—"

"I dunno. He might really be sick."

"*Home*sick and run off! Well, not on my watch."

Craig inhaled dirt, ozone, exhaust. "You call his parents?"

Tim looked like he'd been slapped across the mouth. "Absolutely not! Camp Cross of Gold doesn't *lose* children. We *save* them." He leaned his cleft chin and goatee on a wrist. "We'll call the parents when we've saved their child."

A moment passed. Tim tried to catch Craig's eye. "Now, we're all very... *pleased*... to have you on staff here, given your history with the property." He licked his lips. "But how'm I supposed to spread the Word of God to the next generation if this camp's makin' headlines for nasty business?"

Non-stalgia

"You mean, like before your church bought it? Like when my father owned it?" Craig flicked off his sunglasses with one sausage finger. He either squinted or glared.

The way Tim squirmed, he might have gotten a cattle-prod to the tailbone. "Oh, Craig. I'm sorry. Forgot myself. It's just— Well. Here. Maybe we should pray." He reached out a quintet of wormy fingers. They wriggled for purchase on Craig's driving hand.

The walkie-talkie in the cupholder blooped to life, a merciful interruption. Robbie Burton's voice crackled over airwaves thinned by distance.

"Counselor Craig, sir!" the teen said. *Krrrtz.* "...found 'im! We..." *Kkrrrkl.* "...Jesse. We're back..." *Ffsstkt.* "...Tim's office."

"Praise God," said the pastor.

Craig Kranszler snapped the wheel a hundred-eighty degrees in one second. Tim flattened against the passenger window to see a dozen crows explode into the air as the bounding van splattered whatever dead thing was their lunch.

***

Craig stared at the thing in Pastor Tim's stuffy wood-paneled office. His Adam's Apple bulged. That, or his heart had leapt into his throat.

Runoff

This was not Jesse Drescher.

"Sure it is," Robbie said. The child-sized thing at his side picked at one of many scabs on its gray skin. Robbie tousled its golden blonde bowl cut; it snapped at him with chompers like joke shop windup teeth.

"Stop it!" Robbie whined, nursing a bandaged hand.

The creature zoomed around the room—half on low-hanging knuckles, half on long bare feet. The adult XL camp t-shirt it wore dragged across the dusty floor. It chittered and snarled, mouth sopping.

"You can't be serious." Craig looked to the other two: the girl, Elle, and the pastor. Neither would meet his eye.

"Poor little guy was lost and naked in the woods." Robbie said. "If we hadn'ta found him he'd've got ate by a bear, I bet."

"There aren't bears in these woods." Craig sat down, rubbing his chest. "There are *other* things, though." He dragged a palm across his lower face. "What you've got there is a pukwudjie."

Elle's drifting attention snapped back. "A puppy?" She grinned open-mouthed.

"No! A—" Craig leaned away from the simian critter's erratic dart. It brushed his leg, yowling, and hopped onto Tim's desk. The minister took a step back.

"A pukwudjie," Craig said. "They've lived in these parts a lot longer'n us. They're tricky little stinkers, too. *Mean.* Lead

Non-stalgia

you right off a cliff or into a rattler nest just to see what happens." He closed his eyes. "They… get in your head. Make bad ideas seem good."

The thick hair on his arms sprang to life on crawling flesh.

"They've come out of hiding. They're back." He swallowed. "They're back because I'm back."

The pukwidjie blew a raspberry and swatted a mug of no. 2 pencils onto the floor.

"Oh, c'mon, sir," Robbie said. "That's campfire story stuff." He pointed at it. "If that's not Jesse Drescher, I'll eat my shoe."

The creature leapt onto him, clinging like a koala. It wrapped its mouth around Robbie's finger and sucked the purity ring right off him. A moment later it shot the ring like a BB into the teen's eyeball.

Robbie yelped and fell. The slate-skinned varmint cackled and hopped in zig-zags.

Tim, whose skin had almost drained enough to match the pukwudjie's, spoke at last.

"Dear God," he said. "Some devil's got into that child."

"What?" Craig clucked his tongue. "No, Father. That's not— Can no one see that this is not a ten-year-old boy? What're you—?" He looked at the girl. "Elle, you see what I'm sayin', right?"

Runoff

Elle clasped her hands together and bent her head onto them.

"Yes," Pastor Tim said. "That's right. That's right, we pray." He crossed to her and scooped up her hand. Robbie stumbled over and grabbed Tim's spare.

"We will pray for this young man's soul," Tim said, "and get him cleaned up before Vespers."

They bowed their heads, mouthing silently. Craig watched the pukwudjie tying Tim's shoelaces together. It smiled up at him and pressed a finger to its tittering lips.

"Listen to me!" Craig said. "The longer you keep that thing here, the more havoc it'll wreak. You've got to set it loose, send it back to its people, before it gets its claws in ya' and spreads chaos across the whole of my daddy's campgrounds!"

Tim opened one eye. "You mean Camp Cross of Gold."

"Y-Yeah." Craig sighed. "And more important: Little Jesse Drescher's still out there. Don't you wanna find 'im?"

"We *have* found him," Tim said. "Hallelujah."

Jamming crooked sunglasses back onto his face, the Head Camp Counselor turned to the rusty screen door.

Something smacked the back of his head and hit the floor. At his feet, spinning like a top: a red-and-white fishing bobber.

Every hair on Craig's body—even the mustache—stood to electric attention. He looked over his shoulder. "Oh, no." His next breath whistled in. "You didn't."

53

Non-stalgia

The critter lifted its gown-length shirt to moon Craig.

The Head Counselor scooped up the plastic lure. He rammed through the spring-loaded exit, into the kind of oppressive summer air that can only mean a storm.

***

Under a rapidly darkening sky, the old van skidded before a chained, padlocked gate. Craig more fell than jumped out, staggering and pounding his chest with a shaky fist. Wrestling the hefty keyring off his belt loop, he opened up the iron moaning maw. Decades of weeds and neglect pushed back. Craig pushed harder.

Just enough of an opening to admit him. He squeezed through and shambled to the old fishing dock.

The lake had taken it: green sludge over flimsy boards, barnacles amassed in shin-high mounds. As he got nearer, the wind kicked up. An ancient Butterfinger BB's wrapper hugged his ankle. He kicked it off over a flattened New Coke can.

Thunder rumbled not far away.

Craig looked down the end of the dock. It was still there, though slumped and worn down: a haphazard cairn of teddy bears, handwritten notes, Ninja Turtle blankets. A little handwritten sign: **RIP WELL NEVER FORGET U**

Runoff

Craig arched his back. Something moved on the other side of the droopy monument. An arm peeped into view and vanished.

He hollered. "Jesse?"

The first drop of rain splattered on his bald spot.

Slipping out of his boots, he tested a toe on the decrepit planks. Then a foot. Then he was stepping out over the water, heel first with every careful step. "Jesse, bud. That you?"

Nope.

A greasy hairless ape with a hay-colored monk haircut peeped around, licking its lips with a purple tongue. It curled a beckoning finger at him.

"What did you do?" Craig said.

Thunder clapped and rain fell in sudden, hateful sheets. Caution eroding, he marched to the edge of the tiny pier. The pukwudjie shook its head.

"What did you do?"

THUNK.

His bare foot burst through soft rotting wood up to the ankle. It consumed his foot, wouldn't give it up. He knelt to free himself and a clammy pair of hands grabbed his wrist. Another one of the critters. And another, wrapped around his shoulders.

Several more appeared from out of the water, or through sticker bushes, or over the old gate. They converged on him, piled on him. All he saw was gray warts, blonde locks, green scabs. All he smelled was rotten eggs.

Non-stalgia

He didn't scream. Didn't make a sound except to sigh.

I've failed, he thought. *Like Pop. Just like Pop.*

Hot breath and little tongues all over him.

Might as well go in the water, a voice in his head told him. *What's one more?*

"Yeah," he said. "What's one more?"

No sooner had he said it than he felt himself limping toward the end of the dock. Felt the rain on his face again, the forest folk sliding off his body. One of them held either of his hands, but it was Craig steering. Craig in charge.

He reached the edge. In a lightning flash, black water ignited to flicker green. He reached in his pocket. Dropped the little bobber in: *pa-lunk*.

The floating ball pulsed. He noticed the two letters scribbled on it in Magic Marker.

P.K.

His father's initials.

"Wait a minute," he said.

A pukwudjie grunted.

"Why would I go in there?" Craig said. "That's... That's stupid."

He turned around. A dozen or more of the things were snarling at him.

"Well, it is," he said. The pair that had him by the hands tugged, trying to pull him back. He clamped down on their wrists

Runoff

hard enough to make them yowl, then swung them both into the lake.

"This is so stupid!" he said. Leading with a shoulder, he charged the others. Some hopped out of the way, others he stepped over. One bit his big toe. He made it to the van and a few of them jumped onto the hood. Out the window, he held one off by the face and started the engine. It burbled to life. He put it in drive and backed into the narrow forest road.

Twisting the wheel left and right in reverse, he swept the remaining pests off the van. Once he managed to turn around, he saw a few of them slithering back into the brush in his sideview mirror.

At this point he realized he was still hanging on to the last one out the window, by the scruff of its neck. It hissed and babbled. Without lifting his foot from the pedal, he looked at the pukwudjie and not where he was driving. He could drive these woods with his eyes closed.

"You don't even *have* Jesse, do you?"

The ugly little thing made kissy faces at him.

Craig let go.

***

The only phone in camp was tied up by The Nurse, so Craig figured he'd drive to the police station to report a missing person.

Non-stalgia

He batted the radio dial off of Christian talk radio, found some Eagles on the FM band. The rain let up. Just a light mist now.

Passing through the big brown gateway onto State Road 185, he saw that Tim's "Bible Verse of the Day" banner had been torn away by the storm. Now revealed was a long-forgotten message from the days before Cross of Gold. Chipping, faded paint, in the same handwriting as the initials on that plastic lure.

Craig turned onto the highway.

And there was the kid.

Right there. Jesse Drescher. Not six yards out the gate. He stood, soaked, in a ditch with his thumb out, water up to his ankles. Every few seconds a car whizzed past and sprayed him.

Craig pulled over and got out.

The boy was crying.

"Jesse?" Craig tried to make his bare clodhoppers step light. To be smaller. But Jesse did not give chase—just stood there, thumb extended, sobbing. Craig sat in the muck—*splut*—three feet away.

"I'm leaving," Jesse said. "Y-you can't stop me."

"Okay," Craig said. He picked at his mustache and added: "Wanna tell me why?"

"I'm sick." The kid sniffled in half-steps. "They won't let me call home." His little thumb fell to the waist. Something gave, and he crumpled, knees in the muck.

Runoff

"I puked three times," he said, "and they just gave me a Tic-Tac."

His little fingers splayed out in the mud. "I thought I was gonna barf again at kickball, but my Lodge Leader wasn't there. So I just went to The Nurse. She doesn't care I'm sick. No one cares." Brown water lapped at his little wrists. "This camp's a bad place. So I'm leaving."

The boy's glasses slid down his nose so when he looked up at the man, his eyes were unguarded.

Craig mouthed his words, choosing them first, trying them out. "Are you really sick, Jesse?" He whispered. "Or did… someone in the woods *tell* you to run off and hitchhike?"

"'Someone?'"

"You can tell me. I'll believe you."

Overcome with pent-up childish anger, the kid trembled and pounded his knees. "Then believe me I'm sick! I didn't see no one! Nobody told me to leave! I don't know what you're talkin' about! I just wanna go home!"

"Okay," Craig said, nodding. "Okay. Good. That's good."

After a moment to calm himself, Jesse said, "If there *was* someone in the woods, I know not to go with 'em."

Leaning forward to hug his knees, the counselor said, "Well, that's real smart of you." He studied and rubbed a swelling ankle. "Once, back when my Pop owned this camp, and I was just a camper like you, me and some friends *did* go with 'em. We weren't smart, not like you."

The boy swallowed air. "What happened?"

Another car splashed them. Craig got the brunt of it.

"My Pop doesn't own the camp no more, that's what happened."

Things got quiet. Together they watched a traffic-blocking tractor snail up the road. The farmer helming it tipped his hat at them.

Next thing Craig knew, a little soggy face was whimpering into his shoulder.

"Adults don't listen to me," the kid said.

"Yeah," Craig's chest doubled and deflated. "They don't much listen to me, neither."

"I wanna go home," said Jesse Drescher.

"Sure thing," Craig said. He patted the kid's back a couple times. "Just don't puke on *me*, okay?"

***

"Are we sure this is a good idea?"

A few seconds passed, and Elle repeated herself.

"Huh?" Robbie, bent at the waist, looked up. The basket of rose petals dangling from his wrist wobbled. An exuberant trail of the flowers, leading from the main hall entrance to the pastor's pulpit, was almost complete.

Elle sat in one of the pews. "I'm thinkin' about it," she said. "And it just seems like... Okay. We're baptizing the Drescher kid at Vespers tonight. *That* I get."

Robbie nodded. "Right."

"But then, crowning him the King of Cross of Gold? Marching him out to the Dillman Farm and freein' all the horses? Who thought of that anyways?"

Her beloved boyfriend blinked. "Well, I thought you did."

She wagged her head. "Nuh-uh. And see, I thought *you* did. Y'see?"

The two of them looked through the open door of Pastor Tim's office. Inside, he had Jesse Drescher on a leash and in a Sunday Best pastel suit. The golden-haired camper was crouched, chewing on the hem of the preacher's white robe as Tim scribbled an impromptu sermon for tonight's service.

"And doesn't Jesse Drescher have *brown* hair?" Elle said.

"Whaddaya mean?" Robbie was back to sprinkling rose petals.

Krrzzktsh. The walkie lit up from a tattered pew cushion. "Robbie?" It was Counselor Craig. Elle picked up the radio, pressed it.

"It's Elle and Robbie, sir."

"Meet me outside the main hall." *Krrsh*.

Non-stalgia

"But, sir, we're settin' up for Vespers. We gotta—"

"Just get over here." *Ba-doop.*

Tiptoeing over their floral fanfare, they went outside. Craig had the van parked right there in the flowerbed, butted up against the cobblestone building. The high-schoolers traded scandalized faces.

"What, uh..." Robbie nursed his mummified hand. "What'd you want, sir?"

"I need you to do somethin' for me," Craig said. "Young lady, hold out your hand, would ya'?"

Elle complied. Craig dropped the van keys into her open palm.

She almost dropped them. As a reflex, she nestled into her boyfriend.

"Mr. Kranzsler...!"

"You two take the boy home," he said. "Or I write you up. Understand?"

"Boy?" Robbie looked around. "What boy?"

Craig rapped on the backseat window. From the nose up, little Jesse Drescher's face appeared—spiky hair and big old glasses.

"B-but that's..." Elle spun around. "That's him! Jesse!" She took a step toward the building, twirled back around. "But we're supposed to be baptizing him— That... *other*... Jesse— Baptizing that *thing* at Vespers tonight!"

Runoff

"Yeah, then we're gonna make him King," Robbie said.

Craig's mustache retracted up his nostrils like a startled anemone. "What?"

"Well, it sounds kinda dumb now." Robbie rubbed the back of his neck, his gaze directed anywhere but at his boss.

Craig reached around his paunch and hip. He plucked a twenty from his back pocket.

"Here," he said. "Get the kid home. Then you go out for a night on the town." The twenty slapped into Robbie's palm. Craig put one hand on either teen's shoulder. He pulled them a few inches closer and put all the command into his voice he could. "Make sure someone's home first. Don't just drop him on the porch and peel out, got it?"

The young couple nodded.

"Don't come back for a few hours." Craig wiped his mouth. "Or maybe at all, hell. Things are gonna get weird here."

Robbie uncrinkled the Jackson and stared at it like he'd never seen one before. It occurred to him to give it to the creature in Pastor Tim's office. The thing that wasn't Jesse Drescher after all. He blinked the idea out of his skull. "What about you, sir?"

"What?" Craig was fixated on the open window into the main hall. Inside, the pukwudjie had wrapped one of Tim's legs around the pulpit with its leash.

"You sure you don't want to come with us?" Elle said, but she was already hopping into the driver's seat.

Non-stalgia

"Nah," Craig said. "I'd better not leave."

The Head Counselor went for the main hall—once full of billiards, soda fountains, and foosball. Now lined with pews, a baptismal, an organ.

He grabbed one of the canoe oars hanging off the south-facing wall and snapped it over his knee.

"I'm the only one that belongs here."

INSPIRATION

My lone act of childhood rebellion was escaping Bible Camp. I did not like being taught about Noah leading dinosaurs onto his ark. I did not like that the nurse had poured Tic-Tacs into an old Advil bottle and relabeled them "Homesick Pills." My guts were roiling and no adult cared. So I walked out of a kickball game and kept on walking, right out the front gate. Although I didn't make it far, I wonder from time to time what I put those poor camp counselors through.

Symmetry

Lucy Zhang

    My right eye melted into my face, eyelashes imprinted into skin like mosquitoes suspended in ice. The sclera oozed white and pink splotches, held together by a drooping eyelid that an ophthalmologist had once offered to fix for too high a price. My iris and pupil protruded from my cheeks, eyeball sagging like testicles. When I became only half of what you knew, I asked if you still loved me. You said *it's not the same, but the love is still there.*
    I couldn't see your lips with your head hung, eyes darting to the ground. Only my left pupil can move now; the right stays, a dark dot statically bound in skin, unblinking. The skin doesn't hurt anymore, now rough and leathery but tender to touch. I marvel at how it looks like rhinoceros hide yet when I stroke my

Symmetry

cheek with my knuckles, goosebumps spread down my neck and arms. The coarseness of my face doesn't register with my knuckles like they do with my finger pads.

We sleep on our sides, facing opposite directions. The right side of my face is squished into my pillow so even if you look over, you can only see my nape, ear, cheek—skin still capable of itching and flaking and healing with guttate hypomelanosis, and yet still be smooth to touch.

We still take walks together, but only early morning or late evening, when we know fewer people will be out. I wear sunglasses and a large, floppy sun hat that hides half my face. At the right angle, I look mysterious, a temptress hidden under the brim, lurking from the ultraviolet, unless a small kid walks by, looks up—*peek-a-boo,* I want to say, *it's a monster,* I want to cackle.

A male cardinal perches on a tree towering out of a house's backyard, branches reaching over the fence, its expansion unstoppable. No matter how I look at it, the divide between the cardinal's black mask and red body seems identical on both sides of its face. "Do you think they can tell if some are more symmetrical than others?" I wonder. "I don't see why not," you say. "Just because you can't tell doesn't mean they can't. They've got to look good to get mates." I guess you're right. But now I'm thinking about cardinal personalities, how there might be douchebag cardinals and Casanova cardinals and gentlemanly cardinals. What if this golden ratio, Vitruvian cardinal actually has the personality of an asshole? What if it brings metal chopsticks instead of pliable twigs for nest material? What if it stops finding food for the female during her incubation period? It must work out somehow since cardinals haven't gone extinct yet.

    A breeze picks up and lifts my hat and from my right eye, I catch a glimpse of a world out of the shadows. You react like you've been stung, hand clamping down on the hat, pushing it down on my head so it covers my left eyebrow and scratches my forehead.

    "Stop." I shove your hand away. "Don't touch me."

    "I'm not touching you, I'm catching your hat," you say. "Just trying to help."

    "I didn't ask for help."

    A young couple wheeling a stroller is walking in our direction. I quicken my pace so you can walk behind me, leaving room on the sidewalk for them to pass. I shift my hat so it's not so tightly gripping my head. It's not actually that bright outside, but I guess anything seems bright when you've been without light for so long.

    Pulling the hat off my head, I wonder if both sides of my face can equally synthesize vitamin D from cholesterol, if they can get equally burnt. I grip the hat and drop my hand to my side, waiting for the cardinal to stare down and pass judgment. You ask me what I'm doing, but you don't pull at my hand or try to wrestle the hat from my grasp because then I'd have to twist my neck and stare back at you.

As the couple passes, the sound of their footsteps and the stroller's rolling wheels getting louder then quieter, I stare at the sidewalk, the laces of my shoes, the leaf I'm about to step on, the shadows of your legs. I don't slow. You don't speed up. We walk like that for a while.

INSPIRATION

"Symmetry" is based on my experience burning a small, unnoticeable part of my eyelid while cooking with hot oil. I reimagined how a larger cosmetic injury might have affected my relationship with my partner, who heavily values the image and aesthetics of any belongings.

Motivation

Summer Jewel Keown

    I thought I had grown out of it. Like colic, a mild peanut allergy, the desire to listen to boy bands. It hadn't happened for years, after all. We all hoped it had been a phase, a really bad one, but it was in the past and I could leave my exile on the Montana family farm and go out into the wide world. And for a while, it seemed to be working, at least to a point.

    On my own I didn't really need much. Today, I just wanted a job. A garden variety, boring office job. I wanted it so badly I could almost taste it: the cheap coffee sitting for hours on its burner, the over-sweet donuts a thoughtful coworker

Motivation

might bring in on a Friday, the recycled cubicle air. If there was any way to get it, I had to push through this interview.

He's talking but I have no idea what the words are anymore. They're all smushing together into a sound like something-something *initiative* and *self-starter* and *going the extra mile*. Corporate speak for *prepare to be underpaid and overworked while thanking us for the opportunity*. I don't care. I want the job. But if this goes how I'm starting to think it might, no one is gonna give me that chance.

Thank God he's one of those people who mostly talk about themselves during an interview. Normally that might be obnoxious, but at the moment it's more than welcome. I lost all ability to focus when that tell-tale pressure began to push in at the edges of my eyes a few moments ago.

Maybe it's just a garden-variety headache, I told myself at first. After all, I barely had any coffee this morning, didn't drink enough water, the weather had been close and humid. Excuses, I know.

Any moment now he will pause. "Rachel, tell me about a time when…" he'll say. Or "What are your greatest strengths and weaknesses?" Something from the "Top 50 Interview Questions" article I googled this morning. I'm gonna need to answer him in some sort of coherent fashion, unless I want to completely tank the first interview I've had in months. Apparently having no real work experience is a bad thing. But my family had agreed school was enough to manage in my first foray out into the world. Maybe they were right. Maybe I should have stayed home, or at least somewhere there would always be a screen or a barrier between me and other people. Maybe I should have locked myself away in a bunker.

I'd been testing it, though, bit by little bit. Like last week, I went to Target. When the cashier asked me if I wanted to sign up for their credit card I looked up and made solid eye contact for an awkward eight seconds—yes, I counted them—and absolutely nothing bad happened, except that he probably thought I had boundary issues. If he only knew.

I know that the interview is beside the point now, or it should be. I tell myself to stop being selfish. Get up and leave. I'm unlikely to get a job offer if this goes south, but still, I can't help but have some hope that somehow it's gonna be fine. I try to focus my thoughts on triage, hope that we're not too far gone.

I consider closing my eyes and making my way out of the room by touch. I'm sure that would make an unforgettable impression. I don't want this guy, this potential future boss guy, to think I'm full-on bananas, but there's no way to explain. Who knows what notes he would write on that little pad in front of him.

Selfish. I'm being selfish. I know better than to stay, but finally, *finally*, my life has the potential of going somewhere. I might get a break, might actually be able to pay my own rent instead of shamefully taking Mom and Dad's money each month.

Motivation

I look over his shoulder at the bland corporate background behind him, inspirational words like "teamwork," "initiative," and "motivation" in vinyl lettering across the conference room wall. Do I really want to be a drone in the workforce, wearing ill-fitting business separates from the Express clearance rack to a neutral-toned office building every day?

Yes, actually, I do. I really, really do. Give me the normality of everyday dullness, of a job that can erase anything that makes me so inescapably me. Being me has only ever been a problem. I want to lose myself in words like *market share* and *synergy* and *team-building*. I want to say phrases like, "Let me circle back to you on that," and "Let's take this offline." I want to work late and have the boss nod approvingly when he sees that I'm still at my desk when he's on his way out. I want to get home, exhilaratingly exhausted, and throw my blazer on the back of my couch. I'll heat up some Chinese takeout leftovers, settle in with my rescue cat, a glass of wine, and a crime procedural and exhale with satisfaction.

But I can't have that if I ruin it all right now.

Maybe I should find a job where I could work from home. Or work at a call center, headset on, the voices on the other line across the country from me and no eye contact required. But I can't help it, I need people. I crave them. I've been in withdrawal for so long with the home schooling and the farm that was just me and Mom and Dad and Becky. I don't

Non-stalgia

know how those nuns do it, the ones who wall themselves up in tiny rooms for life so that they can be closer to God. If that's the only way to find God, then God can just get lost. He hasn't helped me anyway and it's not like it's for lack of prayers.

Maybe I can pretend I have food poisoning or indigestion. It would be embarrassing if my potential future boss thought I had to leave because I was about to crap my pants, but ultimately probably better than the truth.

All right, so I can't leave and I can't stay. Surely there's a third option, a way around it. If I just don't make eye contact maybe it will go away. I can control this. I just need more practice. But how do I practice when the consequences are so big? How do those people who walk tightropes between two skyscrapers *practice*? They could never really prepare for that. There's no real way to simulate what the air will be like that high up or how they will feel if they look down. They rehearse what they can and then they just do it.

I'm going to just do it. I am not going to let this thing beat me. Not again.

I will myself to stop riding the tornado of thoughts in my brain and listen. He's talking about a contest they have every year where the top stats earners in each department get invited to a retreat in Hawaii. I don't really aspire to all that but he seems super into it and I let him go on, arranging my face into what I hope is a thoughtful but not-too-eager expression. I blink a few

Motivation

times, ordering my eyes to stop whatever they're doing and just be normal.

The pressure eases a little. I breathe. Maybe I'm alright after all. Was it really just that simple? Did I just need more willpower? Or maybe it wasn't anything in the first place and I was just overreacting, imagining the worst because of all the stress. How silly of me. It makes sense, though. Stress seemed to be the common thread when it happened before. Stress and an authority figure giving me one-on-one attention I don't know what to do with. So basically, exactly an interview. But I'm okay. I'm going to get through it this time. I've finally done it.

Oh no, he's stopped talking. It must be my turn to speak.

I smile and hope it looks like I'm ruminating on the question, whatever that was. *Come on, brain, surely while I was panicking you were also storing his words in there.* Isn't that what the subconscious is for? Holding onto old song lyrics and the words people say while you're thinking of other things, right there just beneath the surface? Surely I can guess at what he was asking. *Come on, Rachel, think.* It sounded like... how my peers would describe me, that sounds about right. We'll go with that.

"They would say..." I tuck my hair behind one ear, pause to give my thoughts a moment to scramble into formation. "That I'm hard working. That... I like a challenge. I'm easy to get along with. And I work hard. Sorry, I already said that part." *Damn it, Rachel.* "Um... I'm good with data and pretty good with people too." That was all mostly true, depending on how you looked at

Non-stalgia

it. The data part, yes. The hard-working part, sure. The people part... there's no good way to say you don't know how to interact with other humans in any normal way. I'm sure he's picking up on that now, though.

But come on, this is an entry-level office job. What do they really want from me? They want me to show up, do what I'm told, keep my head down, don't get reported to HR, work harder than the pay they give me, and never complain. I can do all of that if they let me. Why do I have to dance first? It's like wolves deciding which one is the alpha, but I'm offering up the nape of my neck. Let's do this.

I look up at him and arrange my face in what I hope is a look that says I'm eager for this job but in just the right reasonable amount. And then he's off to talking about himself again. Thank God for narcissism. I try to listen as he tells me about how he started with Butler & Dreyfus right out of business school, and of course he has to name-drop Dartmouth.

What would it be like, reporting to this guy every day? What's his name? Mitchell? Yeah, Mitchell. It's written on the business card he handed me when I walked in, the one sitting in front of me. Listening to Mitchell talk himself up, me the audience. I could be anyone, he doesn't care. There's something freeing in that. I'm not the weird girl. I'm not dangerous. I just am.

Motivation

He's going on about how great their 401(k) match is, about how he could retire at forty if he wanted to, though of course he doesn't want to. He plans to make as much as he can because he's a pilot in his spare time. He loves small planes, especially historic ones. He even flew one to the annual management summit on Cape Cod one year. I'm getting delightfully lost in his ego and his expensive suit and his hair gel when he stops, leans forward, and looks me straight in the eye.

"There are a lot of perks here," he says, his voice firm, "but you have to put in the legwork to climb up the ladder. Do you have the motivation to do that?"

My stomach drops and I blink. Once, twice, again. The pressure swoops back in like it was waiting for one weak moment to make itself known. The lights dim outside my immediate field of vision, but only for me. There are little swirls of light in my periphery, stretch marks wiggling against the air. Mitchell is watching me, waiting for an answer. He doesn't notice anything strange happening, not yet.

He doesn't react as distance starts to grow between us, like the room is bending under a convex lens. I try to look away but I'm stuck. We're connected. Even though I try to move, my eyes are locked to him. It's coming. It's too late.

He leans his head slightly to the side, impatient that I'm not answering his question so he can go back to talking. *I'm sorry,* I think, but I don't say it out loud.

Non-stalgia

I've tried before to explain how this feels from my side, what it looks like, but it's like no one ever invented words that could describe it appropriately. This connection forms, a tunnel with clear, Jello-like walls, but only in my own field of vision. No one else has ever seen it. Once, someone told me my eyes looked weird, just before it happened, but that's the only time anyone ever noticed anything before it was too late.

He looks like he's moving far away, but it's a trick of perspective. He's not far away. He's getting smaller. As I watch helplessly, locked onto him like I have tractor-beam vision, his six-foot-tall frame begins to shrink.

At least he stays proportionate and his clothes are shrinking too. A stray thought inappropriately jokes that at least his expensive suit still fits.

I have no idea why this happens the way it does. I thought about the mechanics of it so much during my years on the farm. I had so much time to think. The first time it happened, to my fifth-grade social studies teacher who was lecturing me about not paying attention, I watched him shrink until he was only three inches tall. He stood there, tiny, on the classroom floor, waving his arms and yelling the quietest little yell.

No one suspected that I did it. How could they? No one had ever seen anything like the incredible shrinking teacher, and they definitely didn't suspect a shy eight-year-old girl of having made it happen. But even then I knew it was me.

Motivation

I didn't tell anyone that first time. Not my parents, not my little sister, not my best friend. They knew I was there, of course, but they had no idea I was involved. Then these men showed up to ask us all questions about what we saw. I could barely get any words out, and my protective mom didn't let them push me too far. They all just assumed I was in shock from seeing what happened.

When it happened again, at the pool the summer I was ten, there were no witnesses. There was just the older guy who was asking me too many questions and making me uncomfortable while I was trying to sit on my chair and read my book. I watched him shrink down until he couldn't even reach the top of my pool chair, and then I just sat there, staring at the miniature version of him gesticulating on the wet concrete. I wonder whatever happened to him. I just left him there and told my mom my stomach hurt, and we went home. Maybe it wore off, or maybe he's still living there on leftover nacho chips from the snack bar, dodging the bare feet of sodden running children.

Mitchell is seated precariously at the edge of his chair, his legs dangling in the air. He's finally realized something is wrong. I can only imagine what the room looks like to him. He probably feels like he's on a bad acid trip. I wish that's all this was.

I reach over and gather him into my hand to prevent him from falling off. He's the size of a gerbil, maybe, a little one. If he fell, I imagine it would be like falling off a skyscraper.

Non-stalgia

"Sorry," I say through my gritted teeth. "It was an accident."

I glance around the conference room, looking for I'm not sure what. There's only the door I came in, so no way to sneak out the back. Whatever I do, I can't just leave him here. I'm not one for conspiracies but I wouldn't doubt that somewhere there's a government file on mysterious shrunken men. I wonder if my name is in it. My dad was an activist in the 90's and had no trust for the government so instead of admitting to anyone what was happening, we got way out of Dodge instead, once it happened a couple more times and I finally confessed to them what was happening.

I should have stayed on the farm.

There's a little snack area in the conference room. Water, granola bars, and… Pringles.

A couple minutes later I walk out of the conference room, my messenger bag slung over my shoulder. Glancing around me, there's no one at the reception desk or in the hall. One benefit of a noon interview; everyone must be at lunch. I don't see any surveillance cameras in the corners. That's good. At least I've caught one break today.

I make my way to the elevator, careful not to jostle my bag as much as I can help it. No one stops me as I make my way outside and into the car.

***

Motivation

My phone buzzes as I walk into my apartment. Glancing down, I see "Mom" on the screen. I sigh. If I ignore it, she'll worry. I slide a finger across the screen.

"Hey, Mom," I say, hoping I sound normal. I set down the paper Wendy's bag I'd acquired on the drive home.

"Well? How did the interview go?" I wish I couldn't read my mom so well. I know what she's really asking: Did I manage to interact with normal people without an incident? She's probably nervously pacing the entryway of our family home right now as we speak.

"Um… I think it was fine." I hate lying to her but what could I say? That with all she and my dad sacrificed for me that I've gone and done the one thing they were trying to prevent? "Normal interview questions. He was a little hard to read. But still, not bad."

"Oh, good," She sounds so relieved it breaks my heart. "Did they say when you'll hear back?"

I don't tell her we didn't get to that part, due to my having shrunk my interviewer down to pocket size. "I'm sure they'll call in the next week or so." *Them or the police*, I think.

I wonder if anyone has noticed yet that he's gone. Did he have more interviews scheduled in the afternoon? Did he have someone at home expecting him? I squeeze my eyes shut. *Do not cry, Rachel.*

"Well, keep me posted, honey."

Non-stalgia

"I will, Mom. But hey, I just walked in the door and I need to eat something. Can I call you back later?"

"Oh, sure. And honey, I know that we were all worried when you decided to go away to school, and then when you decided to stay and get a job, but you showed that you could handle it. I'm so proud of you."

"Thanks, Mom," I say, trying to force down the lump in my throat. I hang up the phone and put it in a drawer.

I pull out the chicken nuggets from their bag and cut them into little pieces on a small plastic plate. I set down my messenger bag, and carefully remove the Pringles can. I can hear him shouting inside, but the sound doesn't travel far.

"Just a second," I say, "and I'll get you settled."

I carry the can and the nuggets to my bedroom and slide open the lock I've installed on its outside. Nudging open the door, I flick on the lights.

"Hey guys, I'm home," I say quietly.

An aquarium sits in the corner, inside a large tub filled with water. My makeshift little moat. Inside the glass, two figures are stretched out on doll couches. I wonder if they're comfortable enough. I've been meaning to sew them some new cushions.

I set the chicken nuggets down inside the aquarium. I always feel weird when I buy them meat. I've been a vegetarian since I was fifteen.

Motivation

But I want my unintended captives to live their lives the way they want, or at least as much as possible. It's not their fault they're stuck with me. That they're stuck small. And maybe someday I'll find a solution, or maybe it will wear off. Not for the first time I wonder about my old social studies teacher and if he ever got right again. I've tried to Google him with no luck. Can a heart take shrinking and then becoming full size again? I don't want to kill them. I'm a kidnapper, not a murderer—and even that is just out of necessity.

My little people wave their arms at me. I know, the pieces are still too large.

"Hold on," I tell them. "I'll go get something to cut them up more." I can't give them a knife. That has not gone so well in the past. I glance down at my left hand, at the scar in that fleshy area between thumb and forefinger. They had caught me by surprise that day, taught me that I could not let my guard down.

I lift the Pringles can up and remove the lid. Mitchell stares up at me, his eyes wide. There's a little puke in the can. Yeah, I can only imagine the motion sickness from getting bounced around in there. Not my finest method of transport.

I take the screen lid off the aquarium and set the can inside, angling it so he can climb out.

"I'll get you some clean clothes and fresh water to bathe," I tell him apologetically. "I really didn't plan for this to happen. But I'd like to introduce you to Evan and Isaiah." He nods at them, my freshman year academic advisor and the

Non-stalgia

landlord of my last apartment complex. I hope they'll all get along. It's not a large space to share with two other people. I'll have to get a bigger aquarium.

They're not bad people, any of my littles. Even Mitchell. Maybe he's self-centered and focused on the corporate ladder and flashy things, but isn't that what everything around us tells us to be? Maybe I'll get him a toy airplane, or... maybe that would just mock him. I don't want to do that.

My phone rings. *Butler & Dreyfus*, the screen warns me. My heartbeat goes double. Do they know? Did I miss a camera on my way out? But wait. Wouldn't the police be the ones calling if they knew? I take a few short breaths and slide my index finger along the phone's screen.

"Hello, this is Rachel," I say, hoping that my voice sounds level and normal. I'm not even sure I remember what normal sounds like anymore. The voice on the other end, instead of questioning me harshly, apologizes for Mitchell's no-show to my interview today and asks if I would like to reschedule. Chantal, they say, is going to finish up the interviews since Mitchell is out sick. Am I free on Wednesday at ten?

I tell her I am, that it's no problem, and she pencils me in. I can't believe it. Maybe I finally caught a break. And I think that maybe, this time, I'm going to get it right.

Motivation

INSPIRATION

When I was a kid, I really did see people get small. I would be watching someone talk and all of a sudden my vision would get weird and they would start getting smaller and further away. I tried explaining it to my parents and other people and I got my vision checked, but no one had any idea what I was talking about. It mostly stopped as I got older, though it did happen in a job interview once. Luckily, the smallness was all in my head. But what if it wasn't?

Heaven's Helipad

Anne Laker

That spring, I fell hard for a magician at the state fair, the sweet way he bewildered the dusty and diffident tots. Saw him *again* at the dinner theater two weeks later—it had to be fate—pulling colorful hankies from this or that orifice, table to table, while elderly couples gummed their mashed potatoes. I coaxed him out that moonlit night, but he wouldn't (or couldn't?) make my undies disappear. In place they stayed.

Tried again with a computer repair guy. Computers once bested desks like gray plastic boulders, beaming monochrome green. Dude came to fix mine at the office. I liked his big hands,

Heaven's Helipad

and the fact that he was clearly an early adopter. Next day I composed a fax, in a cowboy typeface, asking him out. Soon, the machine spit out a polite decline. If only I had used a different font.

But then came the junket. This was when the studios pumped out cash like pituitaries spit hormones. They flew us critics out to Candyland, all-expenses-paid, to bribe us for good reviews of a tepid teen comedy: *Can't Hardly Be Patient*, starring Jennifer Loathe Hewitt, Peter Rivetelli, and Seth Orange. Don't get me wrong, I was happy to be there. A free room at the Three Seasons Beverly Knobs Hotel...heck yes!

With unlimited room service, I ordered petite croissants, eggs benedict, full-fat yogurt, a mound of glistening berries, and hot chocolate with mini marshmallows and chocolate shavings in ramekins, with tiny individual spoons. A balls-to-the-wall breakfast. I was now in the land of abandon.

***

They loaded us on buses to the screening. The stars of the film paced and pouted like zoo leopards in the back of the theater. I would later write in my review: "The hip-hop white boy (Seth Orange) fills his backpack with condoms and prowls the party looking for action. The sci-fi geek plots to sabotage the jock but winds up raving drunk, thrashing to heavy metal and fighting off girls. The editing is brisk. Orange has a spastic face."

Non-stalgia

Neither piles of beautiful berries nor gourmet cocoa could buy anything more than my neutrality. I was never good at quote whoring.

Next came the interview mill, where we reporters sat round robin style and teen star after teen star entered the room—90% of them in black cashmere, a failed effort to look smarter—while fluttering publicists nursed their early model cell phones like pacifiers. Each round, we introduced ourselves. "I'm Emma from Ohio," I said. "Hi, Emma from Ohio," said Seth Orange. He had bulgy, warm eyes like a calf's and loads of moxie. The rest of the actors, vacuous all, had little to say. We critics, crusty and chagrined, had no good questions.

But we liked to talk amongst ourselves. To the left of me was Steven, house critic at *The Turnip*, the satirical newspaper my brother and I worshipped ("Winner Didn't Even Know It Was Pie-Eating Contest"). Steven had every ounce of sass his job required. This wasn't his first junket. He asked me to meet him later. He took me to the hotel roof, to the helipad, free of any fencing. I half expected Beetle-Man or Brice Willis to swoop over from a skyscraper.

As night rose and the homes in the hills went glittery, we sat back to back, jawing about all our favorite cinematographers. His rib cage shifted when he laughed, or spoke of Roger Deakins. High above Candyland, there I was, out past midnight with a

Turnip staffer! He hinted at complications with an extant girlfriend, but why was that my problem?

I was this close to turning around for a kiss, when a tornadic wind whipped and my eardrums nearly withered. A full-frontal helicopter was hoarding the air.

A line flew out! A voice called my name.

It was spastic Seth, coaxing me skyward, into a cloud of affirmative faxes.

INSPIRATION

In the late '90s, I was writing a film review per week for NUVO, an independent newsweekly in Indianapolis. I went on this one and only press junket. Sorry to say I never saw my fellow rooftop film critic again. An internet search reveals that he's now a producer at NPR and a father of two. As for Seth "Orange," of *Robot Chicken* fame, he did in fact say my name. Say my name!

Non-stalgia

Blonde Nostalgia

Christopher S. Bell

You don't want to pick a feeling, not for today or all those that follow. Edie does it all the time. Feeling blessed and hungry. Insert margarita shot or a well-cropped porterhouse. Feeling tired and pumped; Edie and Dee in their vintage tees, smiling under pink stage lights, waiting for the band. Here you thought girls grew out of these infatuations when they came of age, maturing into longer skirts and husband types who only acted like boys on the weekends. They'd save all the ticket stubs and photographs full of new hair colors safely in a shoebox at the very back of a closet next to sex toys and failed craft projects.

Blonde Nostalgia

These moments were meant to be reflected upon fondly, although the first time you saw Edie is an instant better left unearthed. "No. C'mon, you weren't there for that show, were you?" She smiles and drinks an overpriced IPA.

"No, I was," you explain. Age 15, dropped off at the firehall by Aaron's mom; Lucius had stolen a bottle of his dad's whiskey. You passed the bottle back and forth in the pavilion behind the hall until the noise started and your throat hurt. Then inside, hopping around, throwing shoulders to three distorted chords, validating guttural sentiments from your peers. Young love stung almost as much as your head once the spins took. Rushing to the only bathroom in the back, you quickly flushed remnants of your mother's baked ziti as the walls shook out of time.

Hers was the first knock you heard, then a voice like sawdust through the door. "Yo, hurry it the fuck up. I gotta change my pad like nobody knows."

"Just a second." You quickly ran your hands under the water, flicking drops onto the Sharpie-scrawled mirror.

Opening the door, Edie stood with a hand on her hip; bleached blonde bangs reflecting the shaky hallway bulb with determination. Only when she stepped closer did you notice the frosted pink tips on each individual strand, the glow-in-the-dark Misfits skull on her T-shirt. "Get out." That same angelic tone cutting through the surrounding commotion as you frantically exited the space. The slammed bathroom door echoed in your chest. This was how it felt to be young and struck dumb.

"Ya' know, I don't really remember that show at all," Edie smiles, whitened teeth absorbing pink and green neon bar light. "I mean, there was one every week so they all kind of blend together now."

"Yeah, I guess so," you nod with a sip.

"How come I can't think of any stories about you?" Edie suggests. "Where were you when all that crazy shit was happening?"

"Standing somewhere towards the back," you admit with a solemn grin.

"Well, I'm sure you've heard a few stories about me though, right?"

"Just one, I think," you lie through your teeth. "But I'm not exactly sure it's worth mentioning now."

"I didn't stab Bobby Newmier, okay?" Edie grins and shakes her head, blonde strands dancing as if it was all some kind of disco. "The knife was out, and his arm just happened to be in the way of it, okay?"

You're floored and maybe a little starstruck. "Ya' know, I don't think I knew that one about you at all," you say before she starts to laugh.

"Well, it's ancient history now."

Blonde Nostalgia

She talks about work, a cubicle stint in some ever-failing HR department and the occasional night gig singing classic rock in her old man's band. Edie Morello's punk past is of little significance despite her tattoos: hearts and lyrics, nature and science fiction. There's a nod to youth on one sleeve and a tribute to moving forward on another. Edie pretends like she doesn't enjoy discussing each individual line despite wearing an outfit to show them all off. You don't mention your ink, figuring it better she discover those lines later. Then you're surprising her instead of rallying for a time she clearly reflects upon differently and with fewer scars.

Discussing apparitions you both still follow adds just the right amount of spice to dinner. There's something about a grown woman trash-talking emo boys and grindcore lads that really gets you fired up. Edie has an aversion for most with only an occasional dash of remaining admiration. Some of these dummies defined her, whether in their direct actions or lack thereof. You've heard some of her tales second-hand before she rabbit-holes to late-night beer busts and garage shows gone wrong. Your own memories are now mere PG-13 misfortunes best scored to The Cure.

You pay when it's time and hold the door for her, hitting the cold sidewalk, full but elusive. "So what are you doing on Tuesday?" Edie asks, leaning against her SUV.

"No real plans," you shrug.

Non-stalgia

"Looks like Dee can't make Shimmering Sky because of some conference. Do you wanna take her ticket?"

You're hesitant to respond, despite a glow in her eyes. "Yeah, sure, okay."

"Cool," she looks at the ground then back up. "Well, I guess I'll see ya' then," Edie opens her arms and quickly pulls you in for a somewhat awkward hug. You can barely reciprocate before she darts for the driver's side door.

"So great actually getting to know you tonight," you say, quite honestly.

"Sure, you too," she smiles back.

You're confounded. This has been your best first date in a long while, so much so that it's not until after you're driving down the block when you realize what you've agreed to. Shimmering Sky is still out there on the road? A group of three men now in their mid-forties wearing mostly black eyeliner and metal wristbands. You haven't heard their last six albums. The first two are spotty at best in your remaining memory. Too many years of better songs by better bands to fill the larger holes in your heart.

Your copy of *Graceful Men Don't Dance* has seen better days. Despite the occasional skip on your commute to work, you still wonder how this shady angst ever did it for you. These guys were getting fucked up and laid all the time. They didn't prepare

Blonde Nostalgia

you for the hurt, never the kind of losers you needed them to be despite singing to the contrary.

It's the exact opposite for Edie. She still loves this spectacle, buying shots then large pints as you bob between equally-deranged members of your generation at the Hoppy Hole. They've got their manufactured looks; a nice mix of slogans bought at Hot Topic, abandoned by college then re-purchased while thrifting ten years later for nostalgia's sake. You've never seen her green eyes so big as the lights fade and three rascals take the stage. It's loud, long, and whinier than you remember despite Harry B's obvious strain as he goes for the high notes. These songs will never sound the same even if everyone still knows the words.

You sing the lines that flood in unexpectedly, mouthing nonsense for those that don't. When they start moving up through the years, you can't pretend. Edie is still giving it her all. She catches stray glances from the bass player, his fresh licks considerably limp. These musicians know why you're here. It's not to have a fulfilling relationship with the one you love. No, you need to be angry about whatever petty rejections still exist. Fuck your parents and that room over your head. Down with the people who try to control you, but thank you for paying those extra service charges. They really help out the man who booked their entire tour.

You're fully aware of how cynical you've grown, but somehow manage to bury it with enough alcohol. Edie seems smitten after the encore, inviting you back to her apartment for a nightcap. Standing in her kitchen, you consider how you'll handle work the next morning, while she drops the needle on Shimmering Sky's *Peach Pie A.D.* You gave this album to your cousin when you were twenty, knowing full well he'd appreciate it more than you ever could. Edie sways in her living room, chugging whiskey and holding her hand out towards you.

You move in time with her, making note of framed photographs of loose acquaintances on bookshelves filled with beefcake DVD collections. Her vinyl library is a half-full crate next to the classic Sears cabinet model skipping with each step you make. A voice says to hold her close, kiss her gently and whisper something you know she's never heard before. "Can we please listen to something else?"

You don't know where it comes from as Edie steps back and scrunches her face. "What, you don't like this?"

"I don't like any of the music we've heard tonight." You let go of her hand and take an equally-defining step back.

"What?" She's drunk enough to slur a single syllable.

Your heart beats out of time with the stereo as you take a breath. "I mean, I used to. I really did, but now it all just feels so juvenile to me."

"That's kind of the point, isn't it?" She grins before her expression shifts at your lack of reaction. "What's wrong with you? Did you not have a good time tonight?"

"I don't know," you begin. "It was nice being there next to you, but the more I got into my own head, the more I realized how much I could've done without the scenery."

"Well there were a lot of people there who had a pretty fucking good time," Edie scolds you before falling back on her couch. You stand awkwardly in the middle, soaking it all in.

"I know," you say, slowly moving to the blue cushion farthest from her. "And there's nothing wrong with that. It just wasn't for me, and was a lot more difficult pretending than I initially thought."

"Well, I'm sorry," her voice rises in defiance, a higher octave than you've heard all night. "I thought you were into all that."

"And what would've given you that impression?"

"You said you wanted to come to the show with me. You could've just told me you weren't into them anymore or something instead of acting like an asshole now that we're back here, and…" Edie pauses a moment as your eyes shift to the open flip knife on the coffee table.

"I'm sorry," you say, but you've already lost her.

"Ya' know what, I don't get you, but I guess I should blame myself for even getting to this point right now with someone I don't even really know in the first place."

"Well, I can leave then," you say, before standing uneasily.

Non-stalgia

"I mean, I thought you were like a nice guy or whatever, like…"

"Like what?" you interrupt, a thud rising from your chest into your throat. "You thought I was still some sad, angry emo boy?"

"Liking a song doesn't always have to facilitate a lifestyle," Edie states simply.

"I just don't get how you're still into it," you say. "I mean, do you feel like all of those songs about being young, dumb, and fucked up still apply to you? Because if you do, then I really think you're selling yourself short."

"It's not something I agonize over. I just thought it would be a good time, but clearly you're far too cool for a good time these days." Her sarcasm rises as she coughs at the back of your head.

"If you knew anything about me, then you'd know that I've always been very uncool, Edie," you reply, searching for your shoes.

"Stop acting like you're some kind of victim here," she bellows. "You're just some fucking poser."

Found them. "Those guys in that band are such pieces of shit," you say, slipping on the left shoe. "I was literally hiding my disgust for them the whole goddamn night. I mean, didn't their old bass player get fired for assaulting some underage girl?" Then the right.

Blonde Nostalgia

"What's your point?" Edie takes a sip of whisky and stretches her feet out on the cushions as if it's all some show she's seen before.

"I'm just saying those douchebags have never spoken for me. I mean, maybe when I was too young to know what kind of man I wanted to be, but definitely not now."

Edie laughs right in your face, the same laugh you used to hear across the firehall as she made a scene. "Oh yeah? What kind of man do you want to be?" she asks with a drunken grin.

"The kind that isn't a substitute for your favorite lead singer."

"You really are a fucker, ya' know that?" she sighs as you stand petrified. "Just get out."

"There's that punk rock girl I've been looking for. Here I thought she grew up and got lost somewhere along the way."

"What the fuck ever dude," Edie spits into the air.

You grab your jacket and consider what's left to say. She's not crying or throwing any objects at your head. This isn't some somber moment as you zip up and open her apartment door, dwelling in the silence. Edie merely staggers each breath and drinks her whisky as you turn back and mutter "sorry," halfway in the hallway.

"Later, loser." She flicks you off with both hands as you exit and get lost on your way to the elevator. There's a lesson here somewhere, but you're too blitzed to piece it all together.

Non-stalgia

Tomorrow you'll hear all the songs you need, and that's almost as reassuring as knowing she'll sleep far better without you.

INSPIRATION

"Blonde Nostalgia" was inspired by my high school and college years frequenting a pretty fantastic punk rock scene in my hometown of Johnstown, Pennsylvania, and the surrounding area. I got to know many bands and people in addition to many impactful genres and subgenres of music. Like all youth music scenes however, eventually the kids grow up, move away, and forget about all the loud noises that once bonded them. I've always been fascinated with the way music can stay with a person, but while there are some songs that I'll always love, there are also ones from my youth that I certainly can't listen to anymore. Some listeners never quite grow out of the youth-oriented kick of pop punk, despite the lyrics often having nothing to do with their adult lives. Crushes are often the same way. One moment they're all somebody can think about, before they eventually fade. These, combined with a slew of recent allegations against the predominantly male front men from some of these early 2000's emo bands, provided all the pieces for this story.

The Night-Doings at Leroy's

Eliot Hudson

Wading through the gibberish of the divorce papers, I was further annoyed when I had to put down my pen. Typically, when a customer locks the door of the pawnshop, it's customary for me to grab beneath the desk. She looked rattled (but so do half the people who crawl into this joint). Tweekers hardly ever have a gun because they'd've sold it for a score already—or were here for that very reason. But when she turned around, her shivering frame and trembling bones told me I had little to worry about—and I wish I'd been right.

Non-stalgia

She was a skinny, shrew-looking woman, with a patched-up frock coat and large bags under her eyes like Sleep had found another lover's bed. When she came in, I thought the lights were on the fritz and the heat'd gone out again—even though I *knew* I just paid that bill last week (late fees and all). She was a shade hostile, but so is everybody in this line of work.

Her purse jolted so terrible, I thought she had the shakes—which many of my sources do, coming here to haggle for liquor enough to stop their quaking. Then she pulled it from her purse, and it wasn't her hand that was shaking. She dragged out something that wasn't pills, wasn't silverware, wasn't jewelry.

At first I mistook it for a muskrat. A demented one at that. It looked like a cheap toupé. But instead of just lying there, it'd flop over, twisting. Convulsing and almost squirming. For a moment I thought she held a bat. Then I realized, she didn't even touch the hairy thing. It seemed to have looped earrings pierced through it, then a silver chain (like from a pocket watch) interlaced through the earrings in a makeshift tether. It almost looked like a hairy spade from a deck of cards. Only…a flapping one… As she talked, the thing seemed to keep trying to roll itself off the desk, almost choking itself. That is—if it had a neck…did it have a neck?

"I…I gotta get rid of it…" she began, and (well) lots of people begin like that. "Before he comes back tonight… For his own good…" Now that was more curious.

The Night-Doings at Leroy's

"For whose own good? Who's comin' for it?" I ask, giving her a sideways look so as I could better read her.

"My, um, father!" She seemed to have surprised even herself with her vehemence and she looked over both shoulders in paranoia. It wasn't for her father's sake, I could tell you that sure as I could tell this thing was no muskrat.

It looked like some kinda pelt? It was ugly, and hairy, and fat. Almost like a gnawed lucky rabbit's foot from one helluva unlucky rabbit; and it hopped around like a rabbit's foot too— only one that's usually still connected to the rabbit.

"The hell...*is* it...?" I probed it with my pencil and it seemed to flop away as best it could.

"I— I don't *know!*" she blurted with more force than I thought necessary, stammering and shaking her head. I could tell she knew. Same type of stammer junkies use when they know full well where they got the TV or the leather-bound books, the fine china...the fur coat—but she didn't want to tell. She was afraid to tell. But why? And more importantly: "*what...*" as in "*the hell?*" This was no fur coat.

"You gotta keep an eye on it or it'll flap away," she said, putting a paperweight on the chain tethering it. I laughed, thinking she was kidding, but the seriousness on her face indicated I was mistaken. I took the flask and gulped a heavy nip to see if it might coax some understanding from me, but no luck.

Without knowing what it was, and (admittedly) slightly spooked, I didn't know how I could help her. I certainly couldn't buy it. Not outta legality or anything. More outta…well (to be honest), fear.

"Shit," she hissed and shoved the thing into her purse, huffing to the door which she unlocked. By the time she spat on the ground and marched outta my store, the air even seemed more pleasant in the room and the heat had kicked back on. Even the twinkle of the halogen light seemed to buzz a bit brighter. Could've sworn that'd be the last I'd see her… but mother told me not to swear and maybe she was right.

I picked up the divorce papers again, but by now I'd lost both the will and the interest. I threw them on what had been my wife's work desk, then closed my eyes and saw her smile, half tender and half tormented.

As the week wore on, I should have been sifting through the expensive legalese which now replaced the words of our cheap marriage vows. Instead, I found my mind drifting back to…whatever that thing was. Unable to concentrate, I found my mind lost. Then found. Was blind. And had the damnedest time seeing. In that lost and found of my fraughtful mind, that damn hairy tuft kept turning up. Try as I might to read settlement statements, each comma seemed to writhe just like that… *thing*. As though it cast some kind of spell on me. Trash out the window seemed to take on its form. The leaves of my lawyer's office plant flittered just like that deranged cowlick. A loose sock in the washer churning—anything!

The Night-Doings at Leroy's

Well, it didn't take more than three days of lost sleep to figure out I had to ask around about that woman and whatever contraption she was trying to pass off. Wooster's a small enough town, so someone ought to know—and if someone ought to know, it ought to be Merle.

If a dive bar could bellyflop off the high dive it'd be Merle's. The type of bar you can smell three blocks away, fermenting from its floorboards. Where the clinking of glass is as common as a knife fight. And behind the bar (carved with promise-hearts and broken-hearts) sat Merle himself with suds clinging to the bristles of his whiskers like drunks cling to the body of their glass.

"Well, look who it *is*! Long time no see! How long's it been? A year? Heard ya went ter *Thai*land—lucky dog! When you get back?" Sober, Merle ain't usually so talkative; but Merle's ain't usually sober neither. "That ex-wife a yers been in 'ere wit that *city boy* from *Akron*…just don't want ya surprised if—"

I tried to shrug off his questions looking for a place to plant a question of my own. Without being given the opportunity, I decided I had to purloin it for myself, and got down to the reason I came.

"Oh, Rita? Yea, she come in 'ere wit that thing! Damn near tryin'er *give* it away… Nobody'd take it. Gave me tha *heebie jeebies*!"

"Hu," I must have muttered, mulling it over in my mind: "Know anything about her?" I solicited, amiable-like.

Non-stalgia

"Only that her husband's one a tha meanest son-of-a-whores this side a Pittsburgh."

"Really?"

"Yup, I hadda kick him out a couple 'er times an' he puts up a wallopin'! But 'e ain't been 'round lately. Heard 'e been actin' peculiar-like."

I paused to sip my brew so as not to seem too eager.

"Peculiar-like?" I ask.

"Lord, he strange enuf as it is—'m sure only tha Debil knows."

I figured with my curiosity wet, I might as well drink from that tap. I decided to manufacture a coincidence. I asked Merle where she worked, and (after consulting some barmaids, and them shouting Route numbers like they were placing bets) he felt confident about the name of the place. I figured I'd drop in—like any other Joe—for a bite to eat.

The Koffee Haus off Route 83 was worse than I'd expected: greasy, dank, and smokey—from cigarettes and burnt griddle. I elbowed my way between bored-looking truckers staring into their coffee and crop-ain't-so-good farmer types at the counter. Through a window into the kitchen I could see a crone was making questionable-looking hamburgers, and nipping at a quart of beer.

Then I saw her; I'd recognize her walk away from me anywhere.

The Night-Doings at Leroy's

"Rit—Rita!" I tried waving her over despite her either not wanting to see me, not caring to see me, or legitimately too distracted in her mundane shuffles for me to be seen.

"What'll it be," she sighed, as if not recognizing me from Adam. I cleared my throat.

"Er, we met the other day... About that... *thing*—"

"Listen, you want something or don't you?" When she turned her face to me I could see she had a shiner the size of this establishment's silver-dollar pancakes.

"Um... coffee, please... and a muffin." She sidled away, slopped coffee from the bulbous pot sitting on a rusty warmer. She palmed a muffin with her bare hands, before she returned, and slammed the plate and cup in front of me, spilling some coffee on the saucer.

I cleared my throat.

"Um... Rita... I gotta ask... What—"

"Number Nine!" the cook shouted from behind the window and Rita left my question dangling and buzzing in the air like the fly-strips above the griddle.

When she passed before me to serve the plates, I shouted:

"All I want—" but she shook her head, delivering. She disappeared out the side of the counter for a smoke break, leaving me to finish my stale muffin and burnt coffee. It gave me enough time to realize I'd never ordered a muffin in my life before I met my wife... that is, my ex—or, soon to be ex-wife, I

Non-stalgia

guess. I sighed, who was I kidding? I was no closer to the answer than before.

I piddled over the divorce papers, wondering how a smudge of lipstick on a whisky glass could so drastically smear a marriage, then after about seven and a half minutes (the approximate time to burn a cigarette), Rita came back to take my five dollar bill and brought me seventy-six cents in change. When she dropped the change on the counter, I grabbed her hand.

"Listen I need to know… I need to take another look…" I pleaded.

"Lives over in Greer, don't go in the day time, he'll be passed out drunk. Don't go in the night, or he's liable to shoot you."

"Oh," I paused. "Then when should I—"

"Probably about dusk is when he rouses." I left her the seventy-six cents in change along with a five dollar bill, which bought me the address.

The next day, I decided to skip the meeting with my lawyer. Instead, I took Route 3 South through Shreve Swamp (where the County Fair Murderer chopped that girl up and buried her in pieces in '02). Past the Holmes County Amish playing baseball in front their barns decorated with geometric hexes to ward off evil. Past the rusted-out railroad tracks that once brought life to this dead little town—Greer. He lived just below the old Indian mounds.

The Night-Doings at Leroy's

It was a squalid cabin threatening to slide from its cinderblocks down the steep, muddy bank and into the Mohican River. The screen door dangled from its remaining hinge and swayed, catching any breeze which couldn't fit through its torn holes. The door seemed just as haphazard, not even bothering to close.

I knocked on the door, but the rapping delivered no answer. Still, the rickety door hinged open. I peeped in, but all was dark.

"Mr. Leroy?" I called, but still no answer.

I decided I'd driven all this way, might as well take a peek in. The minute I did, I heard the cocking of a shotgun. Twelve-gauge by the sound of it. He had the advantage on me, his eyes already adjusted in the dark.

"Mr. Leroy, your wife came into my store—"

"What'd that bitch want?" He croaked. His voice was raspy and in the dark, I couldn't quite catch his features.

"Well, she had this…thing…and she wouldn't tell me…"

"Oh, that it?" He said, and from the moon glinting off his barrel, I could see he lowered his aim.

"Well, if you could, sir, I got some questions about it…"

"Horse shit, ya ain't gettin' it!" He raised the barrel again.

"No, sir, that's not why I'm here… I can't get it outta my head. It's got, like… some kind of spell on me… *something*. I—I gotta know what—"

Non-stalgia

"Hell, fine. Wouldn't believe me if I told ya anyway. Well, ya can stay fer a while—see fer yerself…"

He trailed off into the darkness and I could hear the hollow sound of a bottle uncorked. He staggered out and started pouring gasoline from a red canister onto a bundle of wood stacked into the vague perimeter of what some might call a firepit, for lack of a better word.

That's when I got my first good look at him.

He wore a mouse-eaten flannel shirt, moth eaten jacket—the only thing that didn't seem to eat was Leroy himself, who seemed to consume calories only through drink. Even his teeth consumed themselves, spotted and falling out like they were stricken with biblical leprosy.

He struck a match and lit a cigarette, then tossed the match onto the fumes which engulfed the wood in a huge *woosh*, which almost certainly burnt the bristles of his shaggy beard. He smiled wildly with its pluming, and his eyes sparkled in the fire.

We sat in awkward silence for quite some time, me not knowing exactly what to say, or what we were waiting for, but Leroy getting drunker by the minute and building his bonfire bigger and bigger, tossing empty beer cans in, bits of tire, odd pieces of furniture, and tattered upholstery stuffings.

He didn't offer me a drink, but I nipped from my flask.

Eventually, he pulled some birdshot from a tackle box. He seemed so bored in the sticks. As far as I could tell (by the

The Night-Doings at Leroy's

myriad of bullet-holes, the lack of a car, television, or even a horseshoe pit) all he did was drink and shoot stuff. Then line up his empties and shoot them. Then light bonfires and shoot them. Then stare at the night and shoot the stars, too. Then all day, he'd sleep off all-nighters.

Once he was done shooting at the fire, he sat back down lazily and the cigarette started to droop slowly from his lips. Leroy hunched over the fire, staring into the flames but looking as though he were focusing on something far away. And I guess I was too…

Then the moon when out. Like a dark cloud had overcast it, but there were no clouds in the sky. It almost seemed like a trick played by my eyes, because even the stars seemed to go out, one at a time.

" 'ere 'e come," Leroy chuckled meanly.

I sat up and looked about. I couldn't see anything, when all of a sudden, a terrible, gut-wrenching smell pervaded the whole bonfire. It smelled like a skunk in garbage. Like Death shit on the floor. Like Bile belching brimstone—you name it. I began to dry heave and covered my mouth with my shirt sleeve to keep myself from throwing up.

There sounded like a thud beyond the fire, like something falling from a great height—but for the life of me, I couldn't see what it was with the fire so bright and the night so dark. Then, from behind the fire, a form shifted sheepishly—I don't know why, but something in my Catholic upbringing made me cross myself instinctively and at my gesture, the creature leapt, hissing with what I could only describe as a split tongue.

"Come on nah! Out wit choo!" Leroy hollered. The figure lurched forward, carrying with it something luminous. It tossed a glowing ball from hand to hand as if the ball were burning his fingertips—which almost looked more like a buzzard's talons—then he flung the orb to the ground. He drew back his hand quickly as if scorched, sucking his (what you could call) fingers, dancing about, grimacing and blowing. When I looked closer, it looked like the moon plucked from the night sky!

"Where's 'e rest?" Leroy's eyes narrowed suspiciously and he lifted his chin.

The poor devil frowned and wrinkled his nose before taking the stars from his pockets and throwing them before Leroy's feet. They glistened like diamonds of fine jewelry and the creature looked at Leroy with searing hatred. With anger and vexation seething in its smoldering gaze. Yet—despite hair covering its whole body—the thing shivered, blowing into its fists and hopping from one hoof to the other like a child standing barefoot in snow.

"Look at 'im shiverin'! Whole lot hotter where 'e's from!" Leroy cackled loudly, standing up with a drunkard's swagger.

He dangled the trinket which seemed to tremble at the end of the chain. Then, Leroy took a little wooden cross from

The Night-Doings at Leroy's

his neck, held it against the tuft, and was extremely gleeful at the way the creature sneezed and coughed. The miserable brute sneered like he'd've killed Leroy right then and there, but every time he looked as if to lunge, Leroy took out scissors and pretended as though he'd cut the trembling tuft in two.

"Maybe I burn a cross inter it?!" At that, the thing cowered back from Leroy.

"Nah, beg. Beg fer yer tail..."

The poor beast almost let out an audible snivel.

"I said beg!" A wild look came into Leroy's eyes.

The poor thing whimpered.

"—Nah, speak!" He said with a hyena's laugh and a serpent's joy.

The thing let out such a shriek, the fire blazed taller and more furiously than ever—the ground shook, scattering birds, owls, and bats from their roosts and into the night sky.

"Well, what ya want him a do fer ya?" Leroy asked, almost tickled pink, but the blush could have been the moonshine in his cheeks.

"What?" I replied, not understanding what his slurring speech portended.

"Well, tell me what ya want him a do?"

I still didn't quite grasp his meaning.

Leroy sighed:

Non-stalgia

"God damn i—*Lucy*?" He taunted the creature, waving the hairy talisman at the end of his chain: "Why don't ya take Mr. *Pawnshop Man* 'ere fer a ride?"

The beast seemed to sneer his hog nose, and Leroy dangled the hairy piece again.

"Want yer tail back 'er not?" Leroy taunted and held it against the ice-cold condensate of his Coors bottle. The tuft started convulsing as the creature grabbed its ass and began running about in pain as Leroy cackled in delight. The creature let out a shriek like that of a wild boar, maybe an elk in heat, or a frightened bear caught in a trap.

Leroy relented, taking the trinket off the bottle.

That's when the creature grabbed me. His claws dug deep into my ribs, and I could smell rotting glands and fetid breath, but once within its grasp, I couldn't break free. Then the thing squatted on its haunches before taking an immense leap. Good Lord—I went limp as a rag doll! Felt myself mounting in the air, rising dreadfully above the earth, and at once we were above the tree line. We flew like a bat so close under stars, I nearly knocked my head on constellations—I squirmed, trying to avoid the night obstacles when I accidentally kicked a star loose from its coordinates so it fell down to earth with a comet tail streaking behind it. I was like a child again and pissed myself enough to fill my shoes if they weren't already kicked up above my head against the sky. The air was thin and transparent, bathed in a light, silvery mist. The stars gathered together to play hide-and-seek as the wind battered my eyes. Through a stream of tears I could see Ohio studded with little lamplight-like distant cauldrons. Then... our house. Or... what *had* been our... home—and I felt my heart drop like that star. Through the film of tears I could no longer see Ohio, I could only see a menagerie of eyelashes, the ticklish glance of lips and delicate fingertips yearning and afraid as I once was and ever shall be. Afraid, not of death, not of our height, but the depth of my sins, and a fear that I'd never again see her.

INSPIRATION

This story was inspired by the eeriness of the Ohio landscape. Hearing hymns from churches lulling over the soft earth and emerging through the mists of Sunday mornings conjured from Saturday nights. Reading Ambrose Bierce (son of Ohio) in graveyards by the waning sunlight. By counting the dizzying stars bathing moonlit Indian burial grounds. A story so inextricably linked with the Ohio experience and folklore I could not have set it anywhere else.

Tunnel of Love

Hudson Wilding

Upon seeing the ride, Ellis realized she had made a mistake.

"Well," Anechka said with a laugh, "this is a bit depressing, no?"

The pair had just entered the oldest section of Funland, where the original amusements sat in neglect: a lopsided zoo-themed carousel, a sun-bleached two-story fun-slide, a miniature train heading nowhere at a maddeningly slow pace.

The reason for their grand quest upstate—The Tunnel of Love—was the sorriest sight of all, even at the golden hour of the evening. The heart-shaped canal rusted beneath flakes of pink and red paint, to say nothing of the filthy water beneath the gondolas. Once dyed electric blue, it had now faded to a murky green littered with floating garbage. Only a few people stood in line, most of them elderly. Compared to the rest of the bustling park, it felt like they'd entered a graveyard.

"Oh, my little bird." Anechka put her arm around Ellis, seeing how disappointed she was. "Don't look so sad. It really was a charming idea. Let's pretend we're in a Fellini film. Imagine the decay feels whimsical."

Ellis nodded, weakly.

"What? I don't even get a smile for a film reference?"

A corner of Ellis's mouth rose. Anechka tended to view films as, in her phrasing, "pedestrian." She only ever watched them with Ellis.

The pair began to attract sidelong glances from the others waiting in line. They weren't in the city anymore, where Anechka's Russian accent mixed with a host of others from all over the world. A white-haired couple in matching hand-knit sweaters whispered to one another at the front of the small line. Ellis could just imagine the conversation: *Harold, they're a couple of city dykes.* She frowned, recognizing her paranoia as silly. In all likelihood, they would've guessed Anechka was her mother before realizing the two were lovers. One of the pitfalls of dating someone two decades her senior.

Tunnel of Love

"Did the park look much different the last time you were here?" Ellis asked, hoping to distract herself, even temporarily, from her own thoughts.

"It looked bigger," Anechka said. "Everything was brighter."

Ellis liked to imagine Anechka as the little girl who'd once fallen in love with this place, barely able to speak English and so new to America that everything still glimmered with possibility. Ellis had hoped bringing her here would reignite those feelings. But she was beginning to feel that such a dream was laughable.

Anechka—adult Anechka, Ivy-League-educated, executive-director-of-a-performing-arts-center Anechka—didn't belong in a kitschy aging theme park. She didn't really belong anywhere but in the city.

"Well, it was a sweet thought," Anechka said, as if reading her mind. "Still, you shouldn't have done all this just so I could take a walk down memory lane. You're too sentimental. It's absurd to pay sixty dollars for entry to go on one ride. A whole evening, gone in the commute."

"It wasn't sixty dollars," Ellis said, the only consolation. "It was forty-three."

"Forty-three *each*? You pay that much, you should go on every ride twice to make it worthwhile."

"We could still do that," Ellis joked. "You want to go for a spin on the Terminator after this?"

Non-stalgia

The idea drew a small smile from Anechka. "Imagine that!"

Ellis did. Anechka—dressed in all black, from her Italian leather ankle boots and patterned stockings to the little wrap dress from her favorite boutique on the West Side—swinging violently upside down with a bunch of suburban teenagers.

"I just thought—"

Anechka patted Ellis's hand as if her young lover were a child, and Ellis fought the urge to stiffen.

"Enough of that, now," Anechka said. "It was a nice idea, little bird. Really, it was. I just never should've told you about this place."

"But I'm glad you did," Ellis said. Learning something about Anechka's past—learning anything at all—had made her feel as if she had scraped beneath the surface of an exquisite cosmopolitan mask to discover her partner was real in the same way that she was.

Anechka's gaze wandered to the front of the line. Then she looked up at the setting sun, her focus narrowing as if she were deep in thought. "Let's drive into Hudson. We could go to that wine bar we went to last year during the winter walk. You remember the one?"

Ellis frowned. Her failure was so deep Anechka couldn't stomach the park for even five more minutes. "Whatever you want," she said.

Tunnel of Love

The ticket attendant lifted the gate and began letting people on the ride again. Ellis put a hand on Anechka's shoulder. *If we're already so close...?*

Anechka seemed about to resist, but hesitated when she looked into Ellis's eyes. "Oh, why not?"

They stepped up to the attendant. He looked nothing like the ones Ellis remembered from various amusement parks from her own childhood—lanky teens in neon t-shirts, or washed-up carnies wreaking of nicotine with blue tattoos fading into their leathery skin. Instead, he bore a striking resemblance to Mr. Rogers, complete with a red cashmere sweater.

Could anything about this day go right? Ellis thought. This corner of the park seemed designed to remind them of aging when all Ellis had wanted was to remind Anechka of her youth.

"Right to the back, please," the attendant told them, gesturing to the last car in the ride. They walked over, Anechka wobbled in her heels on the uneven wooden planks. Between the slats, the water rose and fell in dirty waves.

***

As they sat waiting in the hard plastic seats of the gondola—heart-shaped for aesthetic reasons, but not comfort—Ellis wished she could've brought Anechka here later at night when the park was closed to the public.

Non-stalgia

She imagined the ugly, aging façade of the ride softened by moonlight, all the carnival lights flashing for Anechka alone, all the attendants smiling widely just for her. But even that wouldn't have been enough to please Anechka. Not when Anechka lived and breathed for an audience. If the fantasy were to be complete—the fantasy of Anechka actually enjoying herself in this place—everyone she knew would've had to be there, as well, waving and clapping, as if it were some perfectly unique lifetime achievement award ceremony.

Hold yourself together, Ellis thought. She dug her nails into her palm to keep still, not wanting to cry. The only time Ellis had ever shed tears in front of her partner, Anechka had just patted Ellis's back like she was trying to burp a baby.

The ride creaked into motion. Soon they were swallowed by the pitch-black of the tunnel. No tinny music as Ellis had expected, nor swirling pink-and-red hearts. Just darkness, the rusting sound of ungreased gears that had been turning for half a century, and the lap of dirty water.

Eventually, they came upon the first display: a four-foot-wide lit tableaux full of gnomes and covered in a thick layer of dust. The gnomes danced mechanically beneath giant red mushrooms, like a knock-off of "it's a small world." Whatever Ellis had been expecting, this was worse. A nervous laugh bubbled up from the bottom of her throat.

Anechka bristled beside her as if slapped.

Tunnel of Love

The second and third displays were much like the first—one held a three-foot-long dragon with a cone of orange flame frozen in its mouth, the other a trio of squirrels playing miniature instruments. As they approached the fourth installation, Ellis was distracted by movement in the shadows in front of them. The elderly couple that had been whispering about them in line was necking.

Several more displays passed—all sad and unremarkable. Ellis could think of nothing but how much she'd had to beg Anechka to take the night off work to spend their first anniversary together. She'd bribed her with the promise of an unforgettable surprise. At least that hadn't been a lie.

By the time the ride stopped, Ellis dared to glance at her partner, whose mouth was frozen in a straight, thin line.

As they got off the ride and headed back to the car, Anechka walked fast, not glancing back at Ellis, not even bothering to make sure she was keeping up. They re-entered the newer part of the amusement park where the attraction lights were turning magical in the setting dusk, the bright music creating an atmosphere of play and nostalgia. If only they had come a little later, sneaking in a flask of good Scotch. But Ellis knew that probably wouldn't have made any difference at all.

Across a parking lot littered with little paper cups and wisps of cotton candy, they came upon Anechka's black SUV. For a moment, Ellis feared Anechka would not unlock the passenger's side door, and she'd be stuck here forever, in some bizarre Bradbury-esque nightmare.

But the door clicked open and she got in at the same time as Anechka. Once the doors were closed, a silence fell, heavy as lead. Anechka did not start the car.

"I'm so mad at you," she said, and Ellis felt a bizarre swell of tenderness. *I'm so mad at you.* For all Anechka's education and indoctrination over the years into the ways of the American elite, her English still had a heartbreaking simplicity in moments of high emotion. "Why would you bring me here? Just to humiliate me?"

Ellis stared at the dashboard, wondering what she could possibly say. *I thought maybe you'd let me really see you here. I thought we could share something real.*

"Well?" Anechka said, impatiently.

"We've been together for a year and..." It wasn't until she said the words out loud that she realized the root of it. After all this time, she still felt as if she were being kept on the outside of something.

"And?" Anechka said.

"Forget it," Ellis said. "It was stupid."

Anechka laughed. "Yes, it was." She turned the key in the ignition and the car hummed to life. "Honestly, Ellis. I don't know what you want me to say."

"I didn't realize it would be like that."

Tunnel of Love

"I told you it was. I said it was sad and chintzy."

"You say that about everything in your past," Ellis said.

"Well, everything about my past was sad and chintzy. That's why I don't like to talk about it."

Anechka put the car in the reverse and backed out of their spot. It took a long time just to reach the main road. More families were arriving now, the cars circling the lot for empty spaces in a seemingly endless loop.

When they reached the highway, Ellis felt the first pang of relief. Soon they would be back in the city, back where Anechka belonged, and this awful day would be behind them.

In the silence of the long drive, Ellis thought about her hopes for the evening. She'd imagined that, in the darkness of the Tunnel of Love, Anechka might for once be willing to kiss her in public. Then she thought about the old couple necking in front of them and felt nauseous.

This is the end, she thought. At least it was the beginning of it.

An approaching car cast a white spotlight over Anechka's face.

The older woman was so still she looked cast in marble.

INSPIRATION

This story was inspired by a former boss of mine. Like Anechka, she was an Ivy League educated performing arts center director who had a way of keeping everyone around her at a distance. I found her absolutely fascinating, and fell a little in love with her.

When I moved on to another job, I wrote this story imagining what it would be like to try to peel back her cosmopolitan layers to find something sincere beneath. Like Ellis, I wanted a real connection with her, but ultimately found it hopeless. I guess you could say this whole story is the equivalent of a final, unsent love letter to her.

The Trees on My Street

A.P. Sessler

I knew it was Walter. The rotary phone rang so many times it nearly bounced right off the end table, like the little plastic men on my brother's electric football game. Normal people would let the phone ring a few times unless it was an emergency. Not Walter Capps. Every day and every phone call was an emergency.

"Answer the phone, Collin." Mom's voice came from the kitchen around the corner.

"*Mommmm!*" I dragged out the word.

"Collin," her tone changed.

Non-stalgia

I let out a breathy groan and picked up the receiver. I already knew the nature of the "emergency," and there was no getting out of it. Even if I said "no," Mom would make me go. "I'll be over in 30 minutes."

"Thirty minutes? You live around the corner," Walter said with every condescending bone in his body.

My head fell back and I stared at the stucco ceiling, mouth agape. "I'll see you soon."

"You better get—"

I hung up.

Mom stepped into the hall, drying her hands on a towel. "You going to play with Walter?"

I must have looked like a zombie with a broken neck.

She mirrored my position, but her demeanor was in perfect contrast. "You want to grab a sandwich first so you don't get hungry?"

I dare not explain my master plan:

1) Don't eat.

2) Go to Walter's.

3) Get hungry.

4) Have a good excuse to leave. (His parents *never* made me lunch.)

"I'll be fine."

"Okay," she said, not looking so sure. "Just don't want you getting hungry."

The Trees on My Street

I shrugged then nodded. "I'll be fine."

"Okay. Have fun." She disappeared into the kitchen.

Have fun. Right.

I stepped outside and made my way to the sidewalk.

"Hey, Crepey. Gotta go play with Walter again," I said with a wave in passing.

Crepey is what I called the Crepe Myrtle tree in our front yard. Crepey. Not Myrtle. That's an old lady's name.

She swished a wave back and I looked left before crossing the one-way street. Walter lived around the corner on the next block over. As I made my way up the sidewalk the trees shook their canopies at me.

All the trees on my street were mean, except for Crepey, and Majestic Maggie at the end of the block. I don't know what it was that set them off, but I couldn't walk ten feet without a Scarlet Oak poking me, mussing my hair, or knocking me down. They were real jerks.

As far as I know, I had never done a thing to deserve it. Majestic Maggie let us play with her seed pods. All the neighborhood kids pretended they were grenades. And from what the other kids say, the trees never bothered *them*. I just don't know what the trees had against me. Not that asking them got me anywhere. And telling them off? That was a sure way to get a wedgie, or even slapped. I loathed them, feared them.

I told Mom a hundred times, but she didn't believe me.

Non-stalgia

"You don't have to make up stories. If you don't want to play with Walter just say so," she'd say.

But she didn't mean it. She *made* me play with Walter. I didn't want to play with him. He was just as bad as the trees.

A magnolia grenade came flying across the street at me.

I kicked it into the street. "Ha! You missed!" I taunted them.

Why did all my *real* friends have to be so dumb? The teachers threatened to fail them if they didn't go to Summer School. It took me two lousy Summers to learn my lesson. Unfortunately the only other smart kid in the neighborhood was Walter. He was a major jerk. Sure, he had all the coolest toys, including everything from *Star Wars*, *Empire Strikes Back*, and *Return of the Jedi*. But even they weren't worth putting up with his bullying. But if I didn't go then I'd have to put up with Mom yelling at me to be nice.

Walter was the only kid I knew who was "spoiled." I know, it's a grown-up word, but one me and my friends often used to describe him.

A grenade hit my back. "Ow!" I whined, then picked it up, almost ready to throw it back, but I got afraid. I never knew how far the trees could reach, so I dropped it and continued. "Jerks," I mumbled.

I just wish once someone would see how they treated me, especially Mom. It's no fun when your parents don't believe you.

But even more than Mom, I wished Walter would see—no, experience—what I did every time I went to his house, because if anybody deserved to be harassed, it was him.

***

"Why'd you do that?" I said, rubbing the fresh knot on my head.

"I was just playing," Walter said and lowered the croquet mallet. "Hey, you wanna go to my room?"

I looked up at the afternoon sky. "Probably better go. It's getting late."

His expression twisted into bepuzzlement. "You've only been here an hour."

Right. An hour too long and one injury too many. I went to Step 3 of my secret plan. "Plus I'm getting hungry." I really was.

He threw the mallet across the back yard into the swing set. "Why didn't you eat before you left?"

I shrugged. "I wasn't hungry."

"It was lunch time when you left," he explained as if I hadn't known what time he called. Like I was the biggest idiot in the world, and at that point I didn't even care.

"I forgot to eat."

"Forgot? How do you *forget* to eat?"

"I just forgot."

Non-stalgia

"Fine." He stomped off toward the back door of his white clapboard house. "I'll see you tomorrow."

The door swung shut behind him.

Ugh. Why did he always assume I would show up? Like it was mandatory. Like I owed it to him. But who was I kidding? Of course it was mandatory. It's like his parents were paying Mom to make me come over.

I didn't even bother following him into the house. I just climbed over the chain link fence and made my way back to the corner. I was ready to cross the street but I hadn't counted on all the traffic. *Great.* I should have timed my departure better. Now I would have to go through the gauntlet.

I faced Majestic Maggie to my left. So tall and wide. The shade of her canopy and plethora of fallen grenades covered the Jacksons' whole front yard.

"Cover me?" I asked.

She stood still. I wondered if she was asleep. It was hard to tell with trees. But she was old, so there's probably a good chance she was, or else she didn't like picking fights.

I sighed. "Fine. I'll go on my own."

I thought about taking a salvo of grenades but it would only slow me down. I had to make a run for it. My back arched. Knees bent. And off I went like a bullet.

I ran so fast the sidewalk joints became a blur. I leaped, I ducked, I did anything to avoid the flurry of swinging branches that surely stood to take my head off. I got pelted with a dozen grenades before I passed through the gauntlet and reached my yard.

I leaned against Crepey, panting. "I don't know how long I can keep this up."

She ran a branch in circles across my back.

"Thanks," I said and stood there till I caught my breath. "All right. I gotta go. I'm starving."

***

It was still morning when the phone rang.

"Honey? Can you answer that?" Mom called from the playroom.

I was in the middle of cartoons, eating cereal. "I'm busy."

"Excuse me?"

"My cereal's gonna get soggy."

She marched out of the playroom with a broom in her hand. "Don't worry about me. I'm just cleaning your mess."

I cowered so low I nearly sunk into the carpet.

She picked up the receiver. "Hello? ... Hi Walter, how are you? ... Yes, but he's 'busy.'" She gave me a wicked look. "Can I have him call you back?" The expression on her face was priceless. She might actually begin to understand my predicament. "He's watching cartoons right now. You're

Non-stalgia

welcome to come over and play— Okay, then I guess he'll be over in a while."

I whined. "Mom!"

"You have a nice—" She faced me with a surprised look. "He hung up on me."

I smiled.

"I asked if he wanted to come over, but he said he didn't want to. Kinda rude, isn't he?"

I feigned a surprised expression.

"Well, he said he'll be expecting you. Soon."

Ugh. It was too early for this. Why wasn't Walter watching cartoons like a normal kid? What was wrong with him?

I finished my cereal, but I didn't enjoy another bite.

***

I sat cradled in the crook of Crepey's arms.

"Walter called," I explained. "Mom says I have to go play with him."

Crepey remained still.

"And why do I always have to go to *his* house? How come he never comes to mine?" I asked, but I already knew the answer: because he had more—better—toys than me. "I don't like him. He's just as mean as the trees."

She gave a shrug of understanding. Such a good listener.

The Trees on My Street

"Crepey, why do the other trees hate me?"

The puffy cloud canopy of pink flowers turned back and forth in an "I don't know."

"*You* like me, right?"

The finger of a branch gently brushed my bangs aside to see her full canopy nod.

"Sometimes I wish I was a tree. Then I'd go and kick all their butts."

The canopy twisted back and forth again.

"Well, it's easy for you to say. They don't pick on you."

Her canopy hung low a moment, then tilted back. Crepey peeled off a piece of her shedding bark and placed it over my forearm like a vambrace.

"What are you doing?"

She pressed down to make sure it was snug then did the same on my other arm.

"Is this supposed to be armor?"

She swished her canopy—*no*—and continued covering me in loose pieces of her bark. Greaves, pauldrons, even a gorget (that one was a little uncomfortable).

"Is it a disguise? That's what it is, isn't it?"

She picked me up and lowered me till my feet met the sidewalk, then nudged me onward.

"You want me to go?" I said, pointing up the street. "There, where all the trees are?"

Her answer was another nudge.

Non-stalgia

I faced the trees. Without faces it was so hard to read them. "Okay. I guess."

I slowly made my way up the sidewalk, not knowing what to expect. The underside of the bark was cool on my skin. It felt good in the summer heat. I neared the neighbor's house where the gauntlet of trees began.

I closed my eyes and proceeded.

I heard a swish. I opened one eye. I saw no movement and continued. Another swish. I picked up my pace so slightly. A third swish. I was halfway up the block and no one had touched me. I was going to make it. I was actually going to reach the corner without a single tree poking me or pushing me down.

A strong breeze whipped my hair back and forth, right along with all their canopies, and I thought, "I bet my hair looks just like a canopy from way up there." In fact, I must have looked like a little walking tree. Would that make them mad? That I could walk past when they were rooted to the ground?

While I was lost in thought a vambrace slid off my arm and hit the sidewalk and rolled ahead of me, carried by the wind. *Oh no.*

Two or three canopies tilted downward.

Then a greave flew off and tumbled away. My gorget went next. Then in a single gust all my camouflage armor went skittering across the sidewalk and onto the street. I was exposed.

The Trees on My Street

A branch slid down the back of my shorts and up my underwear went.

"OWWW!" I tried to run and lower my underwear by pulling on my shorts at the same time. It was an impossible task.

I turned back to face a tree stooping all the way down. *Oh, God.* This was it. I was done for.

Two of its enormous branches wrapped around me, lifted me up at a dizzying speed and swung around so fast I nearly blacked out. They lowered me till my feet touched the sidewalk and shoved me. I went stumbling forward, almost onto my face, had I not put a foot well in front of me.

"You guys are jerks!" I shouted and ran back, right past Crepey. She tried to comfort me, but I was mad at her, too. I ran out of her reach, across our lawn, and into the house.

"Back so soon?" Mom asked, her sweaty hair glued to her forehead. I don't think she ever stopped cleaning.

"I figured I'd go after lunch."

"Why after lunch?"

"So I don't get hungry before I go over."

She knew I was stalling. "You just ate. You can come back in a few hours."

A few hours? Was she *trying* to get me killed?

"Mom," I drew it out long and thin.

"You need to get some sun. Come back around noon."

There was no winning with her.

Non-stalgia

***

I stood at the foot of the gauntlet. Whether it was them or Walter, I was going to get beat up. My stomach turned sour and I burped up Lucky Charms. My face screwed tight. I swallowed the bile and entered the melee, determined to round the block, no matter what.

I made it as far as the neighbor's house when I was pelted with a grenade in the head. That was it. I was finished.

I turned my head. "Hey! You hit me you jerk!" I shouted, and cowered in anticipation of retaliation.

But it didn't come.

My back straightened.

The trees were still. Too still. I picked up my pace to reach the corner.

I heard a branch scrape on the sidewalk behind me, so I walked faster, when I got dinged in the back a second time. I spun on my heel. "All right, which one of you threw that?"

No one answered. I looked around and found the seed pod that had bounced off of me a few feet away. I glanced back at the trees. I was about to continue to the corner when I caught the slightest movement among the thousands of branches towering over me.

"Was it you?" I said. "It was you, wasn't it?"

I reached down and took the seed pod. "I ought to—"

The Trees on My Street

The tree bowed ever so slightly.

"—throw this—"

The canopy nodded.

"—at you!"

It nodded again.

"You want me? To throw this at you?"

It nodded three times.

I glanced at the other trees, and each one in turn offered a single nod. "You all want me to throw this at him?"

The whole of them nodded, so that their leaves swished in an almost musical noise.

I didn't trust them. "Then what? You all beat me up?"

They stopped nodding. Some turned towards others then back toward me. Branches raised like shrugging shoulders.

"So if I throw this at him, you won't beat me up?"

They shook and swished in unison.

"For real?"

Some shook, others nodded, then the ones that shook realized they should be nodding.

"Okay." I raised the seed pod to throw it, just knowing they were going to kill me once I threw it, but I was fairly certain there was no escape at this point. I resigned my fate. My hand drew back. I closed my eyes. And tossed my grenade.

I heard it make impact and waited for the assault of branches, but they didn't come. Instead, I heard the patter of the grenade rolling down the sidewalk.

Non-stalgia

I opened my eyes to find the grenade at my feet. I slowly reached down and picked it up. I was getting ready to throw it again when the tree pointed to another. I spun to see that other tree nodding, so I threw the grenade at that one. It tossed it back so that it hit me in the chest.

I laughed. "You got me."

That tree pointed to another, and it nodded, so I threw the grenade at that one, hitting its trunk. It reached down and threw the grenade back, tapping my leg.

For the next hour we played, tossing the grenade back and forth. I even found a few more grenades in Mrs. Stephens' yard. Soon we were all throwing them at each other. After all the running, throwing, and dodging, I was exhausted. I think they understood because they threw the grenades with less and less frequency.

"Whew," I said, out of breath. "I think I better get going now." As soon as I said it I was suddenly afraid they might have a change of heart, but after a moment I realized they wouldn't.

"So what do y'all say? Play again tomorrow?"

The proceeding swish of nodding canopies confirmed that yes, they would most certainly enjoy playing again. So would I.

Let Walter make his own friends.

INSPIRATION

As a child I was terrified of the trees that lined the sidewalk on my block. In my dreams they were vindictive, sentient things that assaulted me at every chance, which gave me reason to make all haste whenever passing through their gauntlet even in the waking world. I still dream of living trees and this story attempts to encapsulate our present relationship.

Cause of Depth

Pres Maxson

From the balcony, the courtroom floor looked small. And I guess it was. But in the tiny town of Wilmingham, Ohio, it didn't matter. The proceedings were the biggest thing in 100 years. And it was all about one piece of missing lawn furniture, lost at the bottom of Sugar Creek Pond.

Wilmingham, pronounced "Wilming-um" by locals, was famous for one thing: it was the former headquarters of the world's #1 geese extermination company. But then the recession hit, and the company went under. The town dried up; the geese came back.

But the trial brought Wilmingham back to life. Sidewalk

vendors popped up. Restaurants stayed open later. The gossip mill ran overtime. And my cousins were at the center of it.

Many of my family members had lived in Wilmingham for generations. Our name, Flox, was well known, usually associated with our great-grandfather's illegal chicken eating ring: Flox's Cocks and Hens. After he quit his job at the sleeping bag bag factory (the factory where they make the bag in which you put a sleeping bag), he opened "the chicken joint that only serves chicken joints." And somehow, he made it 35 years before the health department realized he didn't have a single permit.

Even though Flox's Cocks and Hens had been gone for years, the name was still famous around Wilmingham. That's why we descended on the town for a family reunion on Uncle Dave's farm every summer. It was the events of this reunion 20 years ago that resulted in the trial of the century, at least by Wilmingham's standards.

My cousin, a sweet, naive country boy named Donny Flox, sat with his defense attorneys. He's the one who threw Uncle Dave's lawn chair into the murky depths of Sugar Creek Pond. But, that didn't mean it was Donny's fault. At least that's the point his lawyer was trying to make every day in the tiny courtroom. Still, there my cousin sat, facing nineteen counts of felonious negligence toward a piece of lawn furniture.

The summer courtroom was stifling. Townspeople fanned themselves with the program that included a business card for Tim's Cakes. Ceiling fans far above spun slowly, doing nothing. Sweat trickled down my forehead, more for the fate of poor Donny than the lack of air conditioning.

And finally, after weeks of procedure and mindless testimony by a lawn chair expert from Akron, the defense attorney said the words we'd all been waiting for. "Your Honor, the court would like to call to the stand the last man to sit in the lawn chair before it sank, Jarvis Flox."

The people gasped. The gallery chittered.

"Order! Order, I say!" the judge bellowed as he flicked ash from his cigarette.

The courtroom doors flew open and my other cousin, Jarvis Flox, strode through the door in a Space Jam basketball jersey, top hat, and 3D glasses. Let's just say this man drove the ATV of life with no hands.

"Do you swear to tell the truth, the whole truth, and nothing but the truth?" the bailiff asked Jarvis as his hand rested on a Long John Silver's imitation recipe cookbook.

"What it do, what it do," Jarvis said, with a smile and a wink at the audience. Half the women batted their eyes, and the other half vomited on themselves. Seriously. The stench was insane and it took almost thirty minutes to reset the room.

"Have a seat, Mr. Flox," the defense attorney said after the last mop was put away. "I'd like to ask you a few questions about July 25, 2001."

"Shootski," Jarvis said.

Cause of Depth

"Can you tell us what happened out on that pond?"

"Yep. We lost a lawn chair in the drink."

"*We? We* lost a lawn chair?" the defense attorney asked, between swigs from his thermos of gin and tonic.

"Donny did."

"I was provoked!" Donny yelled from his seat at the defense's table. "Order!" the judge yelled. "One more outburst like that, and you'll be back in solitary confinement before you can say 'One blackbird on an old wire fence, huntin' for worms in his Sunday best, along come Barney with his pipe and drum, gone is the blackbird, yum yum yum."

The audience clapped along as he sang.

"So, do they eat the blackbird?" Jarvis asked.

"Continue, Mr. Higgins," the judge said to the defense attorney, ignoring the man on the stand. "You better be going somewhere with this."

"Let the record show," the defense attorney said. "When Jarvis refers to the lawn chair, he's referring to a bi-fold model 7 with a nylon/polyester-blend fabric from Wilmingham Lawn and Supply."

"Sho nuff," Jarvis replied.

"Please continue with your version of events," the defense attorney said.

"What more can be said? Donny threw the chair in the water. Skippity-doo, open-and-shut case."

"Did anyone else see it happen?"

Non-stalgia

"That's a big negativo."

I exhaled and sat back in my chair. *No one saw it happen?* I saw it. Clear as day. I was also on the raft in the middle of Sugar Creek Pond. But I wasn't about to stand up and insert myself into this circus. I had kids to feed.

"What about everyone else at the family reunion? The people fishing on the shore? The other kids swimming? Everyone around the firepit nearby?"

"Why don't you ask them?" Jarvis said.

"Okay," the defense attorney said. "Let's try this. I'm going to read you some sections of poor Donny's—"

"Objection, your honor!" The prosecutor yelled. "Misleading. Donny is not poor! He drives a blue Mustang!"

"Sustained, Mr. Jones."

"Fine," the defense attorney said without separating his teeth. "I'm going to read portions of *miserly* Donny's affidavit, and Jarvis, you can tell me your side of the story."

"Heidi-ho, le'go."

The defense attorney smiled as he smoothed the lapels of his jacket. "Let the record show that is Mr. Flox's way of saying, 'Let's go.'"

The court stenographer barely looked up from her copy of *Soap Opera Digest*. The defense attorney picked up a large stack of papers. "This is Donny's sworn confession, signed after a thirteen-hour interrogation with injuries and psychological abuse."

The gallery clapped.

"And Donny states," the defense attorney continued, "'It all began when Jarvis kicked me off the raft.' Do you care to comment on that?"

"Oh yeah. I kicked him off the raft."

"How?"

"He was climbing up the ladder after having a refreshing swim, and from my seat in the lawn chair, I gave him the ol' nudge-a-roo back in the water."

"So, you were sitting in the lawn chair at the time?"

"Hell yeah. Enjoying myself a fine afternoon on the water with my cousins," Jarvis said.

"Was it just a nudge, though?"

"Yeah, a nudge-a-roo."

"Right."

"At first."

"What do you mean, 'at first'?"

"Well, every time I did it, I nudge-a-roo'd a little more."

"I see. Is it fair to say you tried to drown your cousin that day?"

"Objection, your honor," the prosecutor said, staring into a brown paper bag. "I ordered wontons and they gave me crab rangoon."

"Sustained. You better be going somewhere with this, Ronald."

Non-stalgia

"I'll move on," the defense attorney said. "Allow me to read again from Donny's confession, obtained by Wilmingham's lone deputy, who is also the town baker. I'm legally required to disclose that his bakery is sponsoring these proceedings."

"The newly reupholstered chairs you're sitting in," the judge added for the benefit of the onlookers, "were sponsored by Tim's Cakes. You don't have to bake if you have Tim's cake. Located on Route 7 next to the state's last Amoco station." The man looked back at the defense attorney. "Continue," he said.

"Thank you, your honor. And thank you Tim for not just the comfortable seating, but also the cakes."

The bailiff, Tim McGuinn, tipped his cap. The gallery applauded again.

"As I was saying," the defense attorney said. "I'll now continue reading from Donny's confession. 'He kicked me back in the water like eight times. I became enraged. So, I quietly swam around the raft, sneaking up behind him. I grabbed the leg of the lawn chair, intending to pull him into the water. But he was too smart. He stood up the moment I pulled. So, the lawn chair entered the water without him. And it was lost forever.'"

All eyes were on Donny. The young man began to cry.

"So," Jarvis said, thinking. "He confessed to not just doin' the deed, but he also claimed it was premeditated? The only thing that went wrong was that I wasn't in the bi-fold model 7 with a nylon/polyester-blend fabric when he threw it in? What are we doing here? This guy is guilty A-F."

"I would never have tried to pull you in the water if you hadn't kicked me so many times!" Donny erupted.

"Silence!" the judge yelled, breaking the silence.

"Not so fast, Jarvis," the defense attorney said. "Is it true that you tried to call in a warranty claim on the lawn chair?"

"What does that have to do with anything?" Jarvis asked.

"Think back for me, son," the defense attorney said. "Did you walk into Wilmingham Lawn and Supply and try and file a warranty claim for the chair?"

"'Dunno, don' 'member."

"Your honor, I submit Exhibit A, a rejected warranty claim for the bi-fold model 7 with a nylon/polyester-blend fabric, alongside exhibit B, security camera footage of young Jarvis Flox at the customer service counter, filing said claim."

"I'll allow it," the judge hiccuped. "You better be going somewhere with this, Ronald."

"Now Jarvis," the defense attorney said. "It says here in these documents that you filed a claim based on the fact that the chair was irreparably damaged. But that's not the case, is it?"

"Who's to say?" Jarvis said.

"Exactly. No one knows if the bi-fold model 7 with a nylon/polyester-blend fabric was damaged. Do you know why no one knows?"

Jarvis averted eye contact.

Non-stalgia

"Because you couldn't produce the chair," the defense attorney said. "It was at the bottom of Sugar Creek Pond."

"I want a lawyer," Jarvis said.

The defense attorney straightened his tie. "Let's get serious about what was *really* happening that summer, Jarvis."

"I'm not saying another word."

"SAY ANOTHER WORD!" the defense attorney bellowed.

"Not a chance."

"SAY MANY MORE WORDS!"

"Eat my shorts."

"IS IT TRUE THAT YOU OWED MONEY ALL OVER WILMINGHAM?!"

"FINE!" Jarvis yelled. I jumped in my seat. My cousin's face was nearly purple with rage. The courtroom was so silent, you could hear the judge shoot a spitball through a straw at the prosecutor, which he did.

Jarvis continued. "Fine! You want the truth?! Truth is, I had my digits in a lot of business deals back then. I trafficked garden gnomes stuffed with counterfeit nails that you can't get outside of Cincinnati. I had an illegal lemonade stand. On the weekends, I was impersonating a dueling pianist for the piano polish, which I resold as toothpaste to members of a traveling circus!"

"I knew it!" the defense attorney yelled through slightly blackened teeth.

"I was in deep with so many people in Wilmingham. I needed the dough. So yeah! I filed a warranty claim on the chair."

"But that plan was flawed, was it not?" the defense attorney asked.

"What it do, what it do."

"And why was that?"

Jarvis took a deep breath. "Because I didn't actually own the chair."

The defense attorney turned to the jury. "Because he *didn't own the chair.*" He pulled a small envelope from his jacket. "I'd like to submit exhibit B, a birthday card received by Bob Flox, another Flox cousin."

The judge shifted in his seat. "You better be going somewhere with this, Ronald."

"A birthday card?" Jarvis asked.

"Yes. It's dated June first, 2001."

"I don't remember a birthday card," Jarvis said.

"Let me remind the court that it's dated *before* the lawn chair incident at the family reunion."

"I didn't write no card," Jarvis said.

"It has your fingerprints all over it," the attorney said.

"Dammit," Jarvis said.

Non-stalgia

"The card states," the defense attorney said, "'Happy birthday, Bob. I'll get you the money I owe you for the haircut you gave me in mom's basement before the food fight.'"

"Yeah, so?" Jarvis asked.

"Is it true, Jarvis, that you *needed* Donny to throw the chair into the water so you could claim the warranty, and ultimately, the refund? To pay your other cousin, Bob, for the haircut he gave you in your mom's basement before the food fight?"

"That's preposterous."

"Your honor, I'd like to submit Exhibit C for the courts. It's a birthday card also dated June first, 2000, but this one's for Bob's twin brother, Rob."

"I don't remember two birthday cards," Jarvis said.

"We've had a blood spatter expert analyze the second card, and it's covered in your blood, Jarvis."

"Dammit."

"Why is the birthday card covered in blood?" the prosecutor asked out of turn. "Is there something more serious that the court should be asking about?"

"Never mind the blood!" the judge yelled, on the edge of his seat. "I need to know what was written on the card!"

"The card states," the defense attorney read, "'Happy birthday, Rob. I owe your brother Bob a ton of money for that haircut in my mom's basement before the food fight, and I plan on finding a way to get Donny to throw one of those bi-fold model 7s with a nylon/polyester-blend fabric into Sugar Creek Pond at the family reunion. And then, I'll submit a warranty claim, get the refund, and then pay him off so he won't stab me at the Whippy-Dip, where I am working this summer scooping ice cream and hitting on chicks. Love, Jarvis.'"

"That's damning," Jarvis said.

"Your honor," the defense attorney said. "How can we sit here in judgement of Donny, when clearly this entire situation was orchestrated by Jarvis? I motion to dismiss all nineteen counts of felonious negligence toward a piece of lawn furniture."

The judge didn't have time to answer. The doors at the back of the courtroom flew open again. I leaned forward in my seat. A stout bald man entered the room. He was soaked, marched with flippers on his feet, and frowned beneath a walrus-like mustache. A dripping, mud-covered mangle of metal and mesh swung in his hand. He threw the object into the center of the room, where it bounced with a "clank."

The courtroom gasped again. At least three people fainted: my stepmom, her boyfriend my dad doesn't know about, and her other boyfriend my dad *does* know about. The stench of pond scum and dead fish filled the room.

"My god," the prosecutor said. "The bi-fold model 7 with a nylon/polyester-blend fabric. If the chair isn't in the pond anymore, is there really a case to be made here?"

"Exactly," the defense attorney answered. "Your honor, I motion to dismiss all charges, and we can all head over to the Whippy Dip to eat some ice cream and hit on chicks."

The judge stared, mesmerized by the remnants of the chair. He leaned towards the bailiff.

"Tim, get the phone company on the phone," he said softly.

"Why, your honor?" The man whispered.

The judge didn't take his eyes off the chair. "Because I think someone's off the hook."

INSPIRATION

Twenty years ago. My family's annual reunion. My cousins and I were out on a wooden raft in the middle of a large farm pond. We were horsing around, and a lawn chair fell into the water. It was never recovered.

Working Title

Georgia Brisco

I wonder if paper plates have reached cool, student cult status yet, or if they're just as embarrassing to serve things on as ever. I stare at my amateur attempt at an omelette: charred and scrambled, mushed with bits of tomatoes and beans.

I'm not sure what to say to him, the boy sitting across from me. Annoyance flutters in my throat – *he* was the lost, drunk one, alone on the side of a wet road. It should be up to him to make conversation now. But I need to think of something because the silence is beginning to wrap itself around us, awkward and dense.

I could make a joke about the time I got a splinter under my nail in the sandpit when we were five.

Non-stalgia

"Do you like it?" I motion to the omele-mush.

"It's great. The beans are good."

He probably doesn't remember the splinter under my nail in the sandpit when we were five.

His face is unreadable. And I remind myself not everything is meant to be written or read. He's probably still drunk.

"So, what do you do for fun, apart from picking strangers up off the road?" he asks.

He definitely doesn't remember me at all.

I glance around the small living room. A ceiling dappled with damp spots, a coffee table filled with paper and textbooks, a juice glass with hardened orange pulp patterning its sides. My housemates aren't home.

"I don't know. I write."

Oliver sets his mug down. "What do you write about?"

I shrug. "People. Strangers. Their stories." I'm aware I sound casual, vague. Is it coming across as insincere? Am I a cool, enigmatic writer, or just a faux, angst-ridden cliché? Are they the same thing?

"And how do you know their stories if they're strangers?"

"People make up stories about other people all the time without knowing them."

He smiles. "Tell me about them. Your strangers."

Working Title

I frown, words unexpectedly piling up at the back of my throat. I pause. He's eager and I'm cautious because eagerness is sometimes just laughing-at-you curiosity disguised as interest. It feels too intimate.

But then, I remind myself, he's here, and it's so late it's early, and he is sitting on my lounge floor drinking Coca-Cola out of my favourite mug. The one littered with gold flecks. Mom bought it for me and most of the time I don't use it because looking at it makes my chest hurt.

It's only now, with a guy who doesn't remember we were friends as kids, when we were shockingly young and happy, that I feign casualty and fill the mug as though it were just any other. I remember going to a craft fair with Mom the day we got it. We couldn't afford much, but I remember a woman with severe highlights selling a mystical sort of glue to stick your broken crockery back together. It was gold, so that if you broke a saucer you could make it into an entirely new thing, a shimmering vein through it. *Kintsugi,* I later learnt.

The woman had made some comment about clouds and silver linings, and I remember thinking that was maybe true: that wonderful broken things were held together only by the promise of something small and good.

"Well, there's this man who sits in the park most days, opposite this weird fountain, around eleven, eating a sandwich. He sits there alone. I think he's scared of pigeons. I used to get mad at him shooing them away. Anyway, the bench–

it's just too *big* for just him. So, I wrote him someone to sit with. A friend." I hesitate.

But Oliver doesn't seem bored, and he isn't laughing at me. He's listening. He's a written cliché, far too interested to last for long, and I have the inexplicable urge to continue talking.

"Then, there's this old lady – she must have the gentlest eyes in the world; they're, like, deep brown and you feel like you could maybe take a warm nap in them, you know –"

Oliver laughs a bit, not meanly, but I frown anyway.

"I mean, I've never considered taking a nap in someone's eyes, but that sounds nice," he says.

I roll my eyes, figuring that's a cooler, more casual reaction.

"Do you want to hear or –"

"Yes! Yes, I want to hear. Sorry." He mimes zipping his lips, throws the key into his mug.

"She sits outside the coffee shop down the street with a flat white, reading the paper. One day, I didn't have enough change for a muffin, and I'm there fumbling at the counter with actual seashells falling out of my purse –"

"Seashells?"

"Yes, seashells, I'd been to the beach earlier that day –"

"Quirky."

I laugh and Oliver does too.

Working Title

"God, I know. Anyway, *listen*. The old lady, she bought it for me. The banana muffin. And she told me her partner, before he died, made the best banana muffins of all time and that he would have scoffed at those sorry excuses. She said they'd had all these grand plans, for after they retired. And then he got dementia, and she had a car accident and lost her car, and that was sort of it. So, I rewrote it, made sure he didn't get sick. Made sure she didn't miss that stop sign, and that she has grandchildren to bake with. Maybe she does. Have grandchildren, I mean. I hope so. But just in case."

A smile plays on Oliver's mouth, it reaches his eyes slowly, spilling over his lower lashes.

"Just in case," he says. Then, "And you?"

"What about me?"

"Your story?"

I shrug. My mouth feels dry and I take a sip of Coca-Cola. It fizzes down my throat almost painfully. My eyes feel tired, the rest of me doesn't.

Maybe he'd remember if he wasn't drunk. Should I say something? It's probably weird not to say something. It's been eleven years, who cares if he remembers? I'd forgotten him until tonight – don't we all forget most childhood friends that way?

He raises his eyebrows and looks like he's about to say something, the words brimming in his eyes, then he blinks, and they fade – a half-thought, tripping to the edge of consciousness, then stumbling back.

Non-stalgia

"Do I have one?" he asks.

Urgh.

"Um. Nope. Well, I don't know."

"Why not? Why don't I get a story?" He feigns hurt, but it's boring because I don't want to tease casual conversation; I want to talk to him about the perks of park bench socials and eyes crinkled with too much love or time or pain or all three.

"I thought your real one may be more noteworthy," I say, trying and failing to sound nonchalant. I laugh, and it's a guitar string pulled too tight.

"Well, how's it looking? The Dude You Decided to Pick Up on the Side of the Road." He grins.

"You didn't really give me a choice. You know, dancing in front of a car at a streetlight usually isn't part of it. The whole idea of hitchhiking is giving people the option to drive by – "

He shrugs. "But then you would have driven by."

I grin. "I'm not sure. The story's a rough draft. I think he's arrogant and maybe a bit scared. A little clever. And I think he knows that, and that scares him too. The usual. It's all quite archetypal. And that doesn't make for a great story –"

He clutches at his chest, jokingly insulted –

"So, unless you provide some original material soon, we're gonna have to scrap it. Before it's a wordy description filled with too many adjectives and close-up eyebrow descriptions and silences and not much depth. Nobody really appreciates that. It's cheating."

"I'm offended. Cheap writing, is what you're saying."

"Afraid so."

"Writer-porn?"

"Exactly."

"Low budget? Body oil and bad, bright lighting and terrible acting?"

"Absolutely." I laugh and swallow a bite of omele-mush. It's cold.

"Voltaire did say the adjective was the writer's enemy," he says.

I raise my eyebrows. "And you've just been waiting to whip that one out casually?

"Absolutely."

Outside, a car drives by, its wheels peeling smoothly across wet tar.

"And does he like her? The girl with the stories?"

My knife and fork thud onto the damp paper plate in my lap. I try to laugh. "I have no idea."

This wasn't supposed to happen. He was supposed to drink tea and eat omele-mush and leave. And then I'd feel good about helping him out, drunk and vulnerable in a student town on a Saturday night. But he prefers Coca-Cola and asking questions that make my breath feel thick and liquid in my throat.

"What about their backstory?" he asks.

Non-stalgia

"What?"

"Their backstory. Context. Surely it's more interesting that they knew each other long ago."

Jesus.

I stutter. As in, I actually stutter.

He laughs. "Callie, you came to my paintball birthday party. You hated it. How could I forget?"

"I hated that party. Why didn't you say you remembered?"

Oliver shrugs. "I thought you didn't." Then he asks, "Does he get to kiss her?"

My mouth drops open a bit, and I wonder, briefly, if he's putting this on. Nobody is this ridiculous and direct and arrogant. Are they? I'll go with arrogant. He's laughably arrogant, and I can't believe I let him use my sad mug.

I open my mouth to tell him this and instead say, "I'll take you to see them." The words have raced across my tongue, light and confident against my teeth, before my mind has a chance to review them.

"Who?"

"My story people."

He smiles. "Okay."

I stare at the mug in front of his grey socks for a moment. There's a little hole near his pinky toe. I push up off the carpet.

Working Title

"We'll go to the Wharf." I say it with finality, and self-possession, which is interesting because I feel like I am being tipped upside down.

"Fine. Then, afterwards, can we go somewhere I choose?"

"Fine."

The whole situation seems to be teetering towards uncertainty – a credulous toddler, new to the world of feet, who just wants to *run run run*. I feel severely irritated and happy.

***

Here's how the next part goes in my head:

Girl and boy walk down – no, scratch that, too many logistics to think about and, besides, it's nighttime and it's still raining – *drive* down to the Wharf. They maybe feed the seagulls from the pier and –

No. *No.*

I'm ill-equipped for making up stories that are almost definitely about to unfurl entirely differently in real life.

***

We don't go to the Wharf – the night is still dense when we get into my car, and there's a police checkpoint Oliver isn't keen on. So, he directs me up steep roads instead, until we're at

Non-stalgia

the base of a hill overlooking the town. A ridiculous, first-draft setting.

From here, the city lights stream together, a freckled luminescent face. There's a dull ache in my chest. I have no idea where it came from and I think that maybe it's been there for a while.

"This is definitely, absolutely not formulaic," I say.

He laughs and when he does it sounds like his chest is full of bubbles. Carbonated. I could probably listen to that sound for a while.

We sit there, and I think that Oliver must probably have a perfectly normal life. Friends he laughs with until he snorts beer out of his nose, and favourite movies, and a whole, infinitely full existence. Does his mom still talk too loudly on the phone? Did his dad ever fix their pool pump?

I think about how this little, fragmented night could be remembered in so many ways. In a paragraph or a sentence or a word: *Yeah man, this girl I used to know forever ago picked me up after my lift ditched and I was cold and drunk and she made me the worst omelette I've ever had. She was . . . I can't remember much, to be honest.*

"You know, you could have been a murderer," I say.

"Did I or did I not get that sandpit splinter out from under your nail with my bare teeth?"

"Disgusting. And I'm not sure that helps your case here."

"Fair. Guess it would have made for an interesting story, me being a psycho."

"Not if you'd murdered me before I had the chance to write it."

He laughs again. And then I think that maybe I should *do* something. Because most of the time, I don't really *do* much, other than focus on other people's *do*s.

"Are you hungry?" I pull out a squashed packet of chips from the glove box. He smiles and says, "We just ate."

Now.

Now would probably be a good time to do something. Now is the time any writer would do something. But instead, I play dot-to-dot with the city lights and wonder how much longer I can distract myself before we all get bored.

"You know what we could do? We could make out," he says.

"Who says *make out?* No one. No one says that."

***

I think about it. And then I realise I should really stop fucking thinking about it. I should stop thinking about wrinkled eyes, and broken crockery veined with gold, and filling up time with words, and everything else in the whole damn world. I should
stop—

Non-stalgia

***

I lean over and kiss him. He doesn't taste like stars or anything like that; he tastes like brandy, and the reason he wasn't keen on the police checkpoint, and night air, and someone I don't know one bit.

I give myself such a fright that I almost pull back. Almost.

We kiss and kiss.

And I'm still not thinking.

And I only get a word down once per eleven breaths.

So it's going to take a while.

But

I think he may have just given me

a story.

INSPIRATION

Something I dislike about myself is that I often don't do the Things. I let them pass me by and then, later, imagine how they could have played out. Rearrange their pieces.

I wrote the first draft of Working Title five years ago. It occurred to me that this thing we do, freezing in a moment, only to rewrite it in our heads later, is a bit like attempting to beat writer's block. That thought ended up combining with an afternoon drive I happened to take past a place where, years before, I'd almost kissed someone. But instead, all I'd been able to think of that night—sixteen and drunk—was something messy at home.

A little later in the drive, I passed a guy hitchhiking. I didn't pick him up because you can't actually do things like that. But then I got to merging those possibilities—picking up the hitchhiker, kissing the person—and imagining the most fictionalised outcome. The kind that might happen if life were an improv class and I was a "Yes, and" sort of person.

I Traveled This Far Because I Love You

Zach Murphy

"The Antarctic cold definitely feels a lot different from the cold in Idaho," Adam said.

"Sure does," Rodger said. He flicked the mini-icicles off of his thick mustache. "Once we cross this next glacier wall, we'll have reached the edge of the earth."

Adam and Rodger trudged on with their overstuffed backpacks through the wintry terrain, looking like a pair of snails with shells full of climbing equipment and survival supplies.

I Traveled This Far Because I Love You

"I really think we should turn around," Adam said.

"But we're almost there," Rodger said.

Rodger pulled out his map. A harsh gust of wind swept it off into the snowy distance.

"See!" Adam said. "Even the wind is telling us to go back!"

Rodger checked his compass. The red needle was frozen stiff, as if it had given up on doing its one and only job. Rodger tapped the glass face of the compass, but the needle wouldn't budge.

"It's so cold the compass broke," Adam said. "If that isn't a sign, I don't know what is."

"It's not broken," Rodger said. "It's just confused."

Adam sighed and rolled his eyes. "How much further do we have to go?"

Rodger pointed ahead with the focus of an Olympic athlete. "If we keep moving, we should get to the glacier wall within an hour," he said.

Adam came to a halt and forcefully planted his boots into the snow. "I have something to tell you," he said.

"What?" Rodger asked as he hiked on.

"I don't really think the earth is flat," Adam answered.

Rodger choked on his own snot from laughing so hard. "You're kidding," he said.

"Rodger!" Adam said. "It just doesn't make sense!"

Rodger stopped. "Wait," he said. "You're being serious?"

"Yes!" Adam answered.

"Did you not watch the YouTube documentary I sent you?" Rodger asked.

"No one ever actually watches videos that people send them," Adam said. "Especially when they're two hours long."

"Then why did you decide to come?" Rodger asked.

Adam took a deep breath. "I thought it would be a good bonding experience."

Rodger squints. "A bonding experience?"

"I just feel like we've been drifting apart from each other the past few years," Adam said. "Like, there's this fracture growing between us."

Rodger took a seat in the snow and pounded his fist into the ground while shivering. "I'm sorry," he said. "You have all this cool stuff going on with your fancy tech job, and I just feel like I keep going nowhere."

"Oh, come on," Adam said. "That stuff doesn't matter."

"I've just always wanted to accomplish something amazing before I turn thirty," Rodger said. "You know, to prove that there's something special about me."

"Please don't go all Marlon Brando in *On the Waterfront* on me," Adam said.

"It's true," Rodger said. "I feel like my life has been disappointment after disappointment."

I Traveled This Far Because I Love You

"You've been my best and only friend for almost my whole life," Adam said. "That's a pretty awesome accomplishment."

Rodger entered a deep stare. "I'd shed a tear right now but it might freeze," he said.

Adam smiled. "Let's go," he said as he held his hand out to Rodger. "Let's get to that glacier wall."

Rodger grabbed Adam's hand and popped up from the ground. "To the glacier wall!"

Adam dusted the snow off of his coat. "After that, I'm not going any further."

"There is no further," Rodger answered.

Adam took another deep breath as they traveled on.

***

After scaling the glacier wall, Rodger and Adam pulled themselves to the top of the summit and gazed ahead. The sun's faded rays shone a gentle glisten across miles and miles of frozen tundra.

Rodger dropped to his knees. "It's not the edge of the earth," he said.

Adam placed his hand on his friend's shoulder. "But it sure is a beautiful view," he said.

INSPIRATION

This story was sparked by my memories of hiking the North Shore of Minnesota during my younger days. While it wasn't quite Antarctica, sometimes it felt like it! I was also inspired by that sinking feeling of slowly drifting apart from a close friend and longing for a much simpler time.

About the Non-stalgia Authors

Christopher S. Bell is a writer and musician. His fiction has recently appeared in *Decomp Journal*, *Evening Street Review*, *Solar Journal* and the *Evening Street Review* among others. He currently resides in Pittsburgh, Pennsylvania.

Georgia Brisco is a South African writer exploring the chosen family, identity, and liminal spaces. She was once in a British TV series and a bad German movie before realising she wanted to write characters instead. Georgia received the UCT Short Fiction Prize and headed a literacy programme before writing for award-winning social campaigns, including Project 84, which drove policy around suicide prevention. She is currently finishing her MSt in Creative Writing at the University of Oxford and, when she isn't regretfully getting involved in a comments-section debate, working on her first novel. You can find her at georgiabrisco.com or @georgiabrisco.

Non-stalgia

Lindsey Danis is a queer writer based in the Hudson Valley. She serves as the Creative Nonfiction editor at *Atlas & Alice* and is currently curating the essay/oral history project Queer Homesteading in the Hudson Valley (hvqueerhomesteading. carrd.co) and working on a novel. Lindsey's fiction and essays center LGBTQ voices, with a focus on fostering resilience and celebrating queer joy. Her writing has appeared in *Condé Nast Traveler, AFAR, Fodor's, Vittles, Longreads and Greatist*, and received a notable mention in *Best American Travel Writing*. For more, visit her on Instagram @lindsey.danis.writer, Twitter @lindseydanis, and on lindseydanis.com.

Ryan Everett Felton is the writer of three novels and two short fiction collections. His work has appeared in *So It Goes, Punchnel's*, and *MASKS*. As a member of the Indianapolis performance art collective Know No Stranger, his work has been produced for stage and screen. His children's book about armadillos was legitimized by much more intelligent people in the scientific journal *Edentata*. Follow him on Twitter @ryanefelton or ryanfelton.com.

Eliot Hudson, a native New Yorker, has just finished his first novel and is currently seeking representation. He's read at the Popsickle Brooklyn Literary Festival, the Edinburgh Fringe Festival, and was shortlisted for the Solstice Shorts Festival 2019

About the Non-stalgia Authors

(Arachne Press). Hudson also performs as a singer-songwriter; check out his award-winning music video "Sinners in Church" (available on iTunes and Spotify). To read more of his short stories and poetry visit EliotHudson.com.

Summer Jewel Keown has written short stories published in *Bikes Not Rockets*, *Pulp Literature*, *So It Goes*, and *Local Honey*. Her romance novelist alter ego, Sofi Keren, has published the novels *Painted Over* and *False Starts & Artichoke Hearts*. Follow her on Twitter or Instagram @TheSummerJewel or on Facebook @SummerJewelKeown.

Anne Laker writes grants, poems, political columns, lots of postcards, and occasionally, a grocery list. She is a three-time winner of Fountain Square's Masterpiece in a Day poetry contest. In 2016, she received a Creative Renewal Arts Fellowship in 2016 for her digital exhibition project [@10000whens / 10000whens.net], featuring 30 years of tiny diary entries. She's also the host of Flick Fix, a movie chat show on WQRT FM 99.1 and mixcloud.com. A recent poem, "Tibbs Drive-In," was featured in *The Indianapolis Anthology* (2021, Belt Publishing).

Sarah Layden is the author of *Trip Through Your Wires*, a novel, and *The Story I Tell Myself About Myself*, winner of the Sonder Press Chapbook Competition. Her short fiction appears in *Boston*

Review, Blackbird, Zone 3, and *Best Microfiction 2020*, with recent essays and articles in *The Washington Post, Poets & Writers, Points in Case, Salon,* and *The Millions*. She is an Assistant Professor of English in the creative writing program at Indiana University-Purdue University Indianapolis.

C.T. Lisa is a person of great intensity and few interests—most of which include books, running, eating, and playing air drums with cooking utensils. You can read his words in *Hypertext Magazine, Masks Literary Magazine,* and elsewhere. You can listen to him in the spoken word & music collaboration TRiO. He is an MFA Candidate at Columbia College Chicago.

Pres Maxson is a mystery/humor author living in Indiana-polis. He's been recognized at the Next Generation Indie Book Awards, in the Paris and New York book festivals, NUVO's "Best of Indy," and was awarded the Naked Reviewers' book of the year in 2018 for his novel, *Pigeon*. His latest novel, *Bastards of the Revolution*, was released this fall. Pres is also an avid musician and a TEDx speaker. To learn more, visit presmaxson.com.

Zach Murphy is a Hawaii-born writer with a background in cinema. His stories appear in *Reed Magazine, Ginosko Literary Journal, The Coachella Review, Mystery Tribune, Ruminate, B O D Y, Wilderness House Literary Review, Flash: The International Short-Short*

About the Non-stalgia Authors

Story Magazine, and more. His debut chapbook *Tiny Universes* (Selcouth Station Press, 2021) is available in paperback and e-book. He lives with his wonderful wife Kelly in St. Paul, Minnesota.

Keira Perkins lives in Indiana with her husband, dogs, cats, and whichever stray animal she's brought home that week. When she's not writing, she gets paid to be a scientist. You can find her at local breweries, running Indianapolis' trails or @keiralynn on Instagram.

A.P. Sessler is a resident of North Carolina's Outer Banks, A.P. frequents an alternate universe not too different from your own, searching for that unique element that twists the everyday commonplace into the weird. When not writing fiction, he composes music, makes art, and strives to connect with his inner genius.

Hudson Wilding hails from Upstate New York, where she spends most of the year waiting for October. Her stories have previously been published in *Foglifter*, *Menacing Hedge*, and *The Dread Machine*, among other literary journals. More of her work is forthcoming in *Corvid Queen*. You can follow her on Twitter @HudsonWilding.

Non-stalgia

Lucy Zhang writes, codes, and watches anime. Her work has appeared or is forthcoming in *Contrary*, *DIAGRAM*, *Hobart*, *Jellyfish Review*, *New Orleans Review*, *The Offing*, *Passages North*, *The Portland Review*, *The Rumpus*, *West Branch*, and elsewhere. Her work is included in *Best Microfiction 2021* and *Best Small Fictions 2021*, was a finalist in *Best of the Net 2020* and longlisted in the *Wigleaf* Top 50. Find her at kowaretasekai.wordpress.com or on Twitter @Dango_Ramen.